A LIFE OF YOUR OWN
and other stories

A magnificent gathering [...] hed in *Collection Three* – the [...] thy of preserving in 'collected f[...]

'How supremely readabl[...]

'Full of good things . . [...] lity to communicate his deep u[...]
SHEFFIELD MORNING TELEGRAPH

'O'Connor loved and understood his country and her people with generous fervour . . .' WESTERN DAILY PRESS

Masculine Protest and other stories, also available in Pan Books, contains the balance of the stories originally published in *Collection Three*.

Born in 1903, in Cork, Frank O'Connor had no formal education and his only real ambition was to become a writer. Aged twelve, he began to prepare a collected edition of his own works and, having learnt to speak Gaelic while very young, he studied his native poetry, music and legends. His literary career began with the translation of one of Du Bellay's sonnets into Gaelic.

On release from imprisonment by the Free State Government for his part in the Civil War, O'Connor won a prize for his study of Turgenev and subsequently had poetry, stories and translations published in the *Irish Statesman*. He caused great consternation in his native city by producing plays by Ibsen and Chekhov: a local clergyman remarked that the producer 'would go down in posterity at the head of the pagan Dublin muses', and ladies in the local literary society threatened to resign when he mentioned the name of James Joyce. By profession O'Connor was a librarian and his other great interest was music, Mozart and the Irish composer Carolan being his favourites. He will long be remembered for his collections of short stories. Frank O'Connor died in March 1966.

The cover photograph shows Shandon Street, Cork

Also by Frank O'Connor in Pan Books

Frank O'Connor

A LIFE
OF YOUR OWN
and other stories from Collection Three

Pan Books in association with
Macmillan London

First published 1969 in *Collection Three* by Macmillan and Company Ltd
This edition (being the first part of the stories contained in *Collection Three*)
published 1972 by Pan Books Ltd, Cavaye Place, London SW10 9PG
in association with Macmillan London Ltd
3rd printing 1982
Copyright Harriet O'Donovan 1952, 1957, 1958,
1960, 1961, 1965, 1966, 1967
ISBN 0 330 02932 0

Printed and bound in Great Britain by
Cox & Wyman Ltd, Reading

CONTENTS

FOREWORD

FOR Frank O'Connor the most important single element in any story was its design. It might be years between the moment of recognizing a theme and finding the one right shape for it – this was the hard, painful work – the writing he did in his head. But once he had the essential bony structure firmly in place he could begin to enjoy the story – to start 'tinkering' with it. It was this 'tinkering' which produced dozens of versions of the same story. The basic design never changed, but in each new version light would be thrown in a different way on a different place. Frank O'Connor did this kind of rewriting endlessly – as he admits in the Introduction to *Collection Two*, he frequently continued it even after a story had been published. Though this confused and sometimes annoyed editors, reviewers and bibliographers, the multiplicity of versions was never a problem to him. When there were enough stories to form a new collection he didn't start trying to choose between the many extant versions of them – he simply sat down and prepared to rewrite every story he wanted in the book.

That particular rewriting was directed towards a definite aim – which was to give a book of stories the feeling of being a unity rather than a grab bag. He believed that stories – if arranged in an 'ideal ambience' – could strengthen and illuminate each other. This unity was only partly preconceived, he continued to create it as he went along. He never wrote a story specifically to fit into a gap in a book – nor did he change names or locations to give superficial unity. Rather it was as though the stories were bits of a mosaic which could be arranged harmoniously so that the pattern they made together reflected the light which each cast separately. Ultimately this unity probably sprang from his basic conviction that the writer was not simply an observer: 'I can't write about something I don't admire – it goes back to the old concept of the celebration: you celebrate the hero, an idea.'

This means, of course, that Frank O'Connor had very definite ideas about the contents and arrangements of each new book of stories. If he had lived, this might have been a different book. As it is, I have had to choose, not only which and how many stories to include, but also which of the many versions of each story to print. There was also the problem of that 'ideal ambience' and the comfort of the knowledge that even his own 'ideal ambience would be shattered by the time the book appears'.

I do not doubt that I shall have to answer to the author for each of these decisions. But for the stories themselves no one need answer. They are pure Frank O'Connor.

HARRIET O'DONOVAN (MRS FRANK O'CONNOR)

ACKNOWLEDGEMENTS

Acknowledgements are due to the following publications, in which these stories first appeared: *Harper's Bazaar, John Bull, Mademoiselle, New Yorker, Penguin New Writing, Saturday Evening Post, Woman's Day.*

A LIFE OF YOUR OWN

JANE HARTY, the chemist, lived alone in a little bungalow
on the outskirts of the town. She had long ago decided that it
was the only way to live a life of her own. In a city you
could be one of a group without adopting its standards, but
girls who took lodgings in the town accepted a discipline
stricter than that of home.

She could not live that way, and after her parents' death
and her brother's departure for London, she gave up trying.
She ran a battered old car and went off on free weekends by
herself, without telling anyone except the Sullivans where
she was going. They were her only friends in town. Celia
had been to school with her and had married the headmaster
of the Technical School. When she got a fit of the blues she
merely packed her bag and went to stay with them, and
they never asked any questions.

The bungalow wasn't very comfortable, and she could
afford to have a cleaning woman in only once a week, but it
had a garden and a bit of a view, and she could live better in
the town than in Dublin, where she would only be a non-
entity. The poor people feared and distrusted doctors, and
they came to her with their troubles, domestic and medical.
They knew she didn't mind tramping down to a dirty cottage at night with a prescription, or looking at a sick child or
arguing with a drunken husband. She was one of themselves.
Of course, they knew things about her as well. They had
known her parents, and knew she was looked on as a bit of a
freak by the swanky people, all because she wouldn't play
the game and fell in love with unsuitable men. Unsuitable

men seemed to be the price you had to pay for trying to live a life of your own.

One night she came back from Dublin, and when she opened the door of the bungalow she felt a sudden stab of fear. She stepped back and asked angrily, 'Is there somebody there?' There was no reply, and she muttered to herself, 'You're getting neurotic, Harty.' She went in and turned on the light in the sitting room. One glance was enough to show that it wasn't nerves. Through the open door of the bedroom she could see clothes scattered on the floor. How anybody got in she didn't know, but the key was under the mat, and in fact anyone could have done it. She searched the two rooms and the kitchen but found nothing missing. Yet it gave her a sick and desolate feeling, like the touch of something dirty.

Next morning she went to the police station and made her complaint to the sergeant, a beefy, boozy man by the name of Lenihan.

'Ah, it's them kids again, Miss Harty,' he said gloomily.

'What kids are they, Joe?'

'That rough gang down the River Road,' he said. 'They didn't take anything?'

'Not that I could see.'

'Pity about that,' he said moodily. 'If there was anything taken we could keep an eye out for it. Young Humphreys lives up your way. I'll tell him to watch for anyone going in that direction. In the meantime, you'd better leave word with us when you're away.'

'For God's sake!' Ned Sullivan drawled when she told him and his wife about it that night. 'When one of them leaves the barrack they hear his boots at the other side of town. I'll have a word with a couple of the kids. The best way of keeping kids from being juvenile delinquents is to turn them into policemen.'

Sullivan was like that; ugly, attractive, slow-moving and cynical, and Jane squirmed when Celia talked to him, because it was clear that she didn't realize how remarkable he was.

But neither the police nor the Technical School kids were round when the intruder came again. Jane arrived home on Sunday night from Galway. The first glance was enough to show that her visitor was no child. She felt sick again, but this time anger got the upper hand. She drove back to Humphreys' house, which was on a terrace by the main road. Madge Humphreys answered the door. She was a school-teacher, who was supposed to read what she called 'the clawsicks' to her family each evening till their spirit was broken. She told Jane her husband was out, and that she had better report to the barrack, but at that very moment Humphreys appeared, a tall, big-boned young man, grinning and pulling on his jacket. 'Ah, Madge, a policeman is never off duty,' he said. 'I might as well go and see what's up.'

When Jane showed him the living-room he said softly, 'Oh, Chrisht!' In the kitchen doorway he halted. 'These yours?' he asked, nodding to the tea things, and she shook her head, anger giving way to hopelessness. She had merely tried to have a life of her own, and even this was being denied her. 'Better check and see is anything missing from the bedroom,' he said, and she preceded him, looking help-lessly round. 'Try your clothes first,' he said gently, and she began to fold them and put them back. Humphreys sat down and lit a cigarette.

'Well?' he asked, and she burst into a loud angry laugh.

'Nothing I can see only a pair of pants,' she said roughly, and then, catching the startled look on his face, realized the significance of what she had said.

'Better make sure of it,' he said, and she checked again.

'They're gone all right,' she said. 'Frilly ones – they were a present. I wouldn't wear the blooming things.'

'That's bad,' he said, and went back to the living room.

'You'll have a drink as you're here,' she said.

'I'd better not,' he said with a boyish grin. 'It's Madge. She starts getting nervous when I'm out.'

'I'm going to have one anyway,' said Jane, knowing well what it was Madge got nervous of – another woman who might talk to him about some things beside 'the claw-sicks'.

'Tell me, do you remember was any fellow annoying you?' he asked.

'Nobody,' she said. 'Unless that fellow on the phone.'

'Oh, was he after you too?' Humphreys asked with interest. 'That's someone I'd like to lay my hands on some time. What did you do?'

'What could I do?' she asked, taking her drink. 'The first time I was so appalled, I listened. It's funny; I suppose it's like being hypnotized. After it, you start to get sick. I never knew people could be like that. The second time I did what Ned Sullivan told me, and he's left me alone since then.'

'What was that?'

'Oh, I told him he was a very sick man and that he should get treatment at once.' She gave an engaging grin. 'You know – Dr Harty, the well-known nerve specialist, giving a free opinion and wondering all the time when she'll start screaming.'

'Was he cross?'

'Leppin' mad.'

'That was clever of Ned Sullivan,' said Humphreys. 'But I don't think it's the same man. This is probably someone you know quite well. Any idea who it could be?'

'Not a notion.'

'Someone who comes into the shop for small things you'd expect his mother or sister to get for him?' he asked shrewdly.

'I can't think of a soul,' she said offhandedly. 'Anybody that isn't normal, I mean.'

'They all look normal enough to begin with,' he said grimly. 'They won't look so normal in five years' time. If you think of anyone let me know ... The bloody house is probably full of fingerprints,' he added gloomily. 'For all the good they'd do us.'

As he was leaving he studied the lock and said, 'I think I'd get a new lock for the door. And you might as well get a spare key and leave it at the barrack. I could drop in some evening and see if he'd come. Anyway, you'd better call at the barrack tomorrow and have a word with the super-intendent. Not that he'll know more than I do, but it might make things easier for us.'

She did as he advised and understood what he meant. The superintendent was a bright and cheerful young man who was obviously much happier with papers than with people. Papers didn't answer back in the same way.

'We could all be killed in our beds, and 'twould only make an interesting statistic for that idiot,' she said to the Sul-livans.

'You're in no danger like that,' Ned said thoughtfully. 'That fellow won't come near the place as long as you're there. He's still too shy. You'll find there's a loving Irish mother in the background who takes him to Confession her-self every Saturday and writes out a list of his sins for him, the way he won't forget. He may get dangerous, but it won't be for a long time yet, and it won't be over you. Damn it, I feel I ought to be able to go for a walk and put my hand on him! You'll have to think of someone like that, Jan.'

'Ah, for God's sake, I'd have to think of half the town,' she said jokingly, but he didn't smile.

'You would, you would, but this is something different. Lord God, it's unknown the lives people have to lead in towns like this!' he added, growing bitter himself.

It was after that she began to crack. Two or three times she stopped the car outside the gate and blew the horn to warn the intruder. Now she had almost a horror of seeing him, for fear she might know who he was. And once more she returned from a weekend and saw that he had been there. He must have come before darkness fell for he had taken down a few of her books. In the bedroom there was the same childish disorder of clothes, but written in lipstick over her bed were the words 'I love you'.

She called the guards station and Humphreys answered.

'All right, all right,' he said quickly. 'Don't touch anything. Somebody will be along in a minute. And meantime, don't worry. You're all right.'

'Would you ask whoever is coming to tell Ned Sullivan?' she asked and was slightly shocked after she had said it. But Ned was the only one she wanted to talk to now.

It was Lenihan who came and inspected the house. Ned came after him, walking slowly. Lenihan exasperated her, examining locks and window-catches.

'This is how he got in all right,' he said sagaciously, indicating the catch on the bedroom window. 'That catch is too easy to open. Blast him anyway! He doesn't miss much.'

' 'Tis nice to know how he got in,' Ned said sarcastically. 'It would be more practical if we knew how to keep him out.'

'Oh, we'll get him yet, Mr Sullivan,' said Lenihan, shaking his head over it. 'He'll come too often, the way they all do. But if I was you, Miss Harty, I wouldn't bother my head about him. Sure, he's only a poor harmless ould sexual maniac. The country is full of them. So long as he wouldn't take anything valuable.'

'I haven't anything valuable for him to take,' she replied.

'No. Only your peace of mind,' Ned said shortly.

When Lenihan had gone he gave a sigh.

'It's no use relying on those fellows,' he said. 'They have no notion who that fellow is. Either that, or they know and they're not telling. It could be somebody that they don't want to make a fuss about. But they're right enough about the danger. They don't see the real danger you're in.'

'What danger?' she asked curiously.

'That fellow would drive you as mad as himself,' Ned said flatly. ' 'Twould be like living with a ghost. It gives me the horrors, not to mind you. I'm going to get myself a drink if you have one.'

'Do you really think they know?' she asked as he got the tumblers.

'They may. This is probably someone you saw being picked on or ignored some place and made a fuss of. Or you stopped and gave him a lift. It was probably the first time a woman treated him as a human being, and it went to the poor devil's head.' He glanced at her inquiringly, but her face was a blank, and he knew that this was what she did normally and that it would have made no impression on her mind. 'Oh, how the hell do I know? But you'd better start making plans to get out.'

'Out?'

'You can't stay here.'

'But where am I to go?'

'Somewhere they won't notice your seven-league boots,' he replied with mournful humour. 'You have them all frightened: Humphreys' wife is frightened, Lenihan is frightened; you probably scared the wits out of the superintendent as well. I'll hear it all in due course, in Slattery's pub. Sex is a game, girl,' he said almost angrily. 'You have to play a three to beat a two, but you play your ace every time. You simply can't afford to live naturally in a place like this.'

'That's a comforting thought,' she replied bitterly. 'In that case you'd better go home to Celia, quick. She'll be wondering what happened to you.'

'She won't. She told me I was to spend the night or bring you back with me.'

Anger was Jane's first response. It was as though Celia were condescending to him. And then she realized how unfair she was. Celia was merely showing that she knew the gossip and didn't care.

'Tell Celia I'd go back with you if I could,' she said with a sob. 'If I gave in now I'd never sleep here alone again.'

'And do you intend to go on staying here alone?' he asked.

'But where else have I to go, Ned?'

'Go to Dublin, go to London, get to hell out of this!' he

cried. 'And God knows I'm not saying that for my own
sake.'

It was as though her tears had been waiting for the words.
He took her in his arms and patted her awkwardly. 'I know,
love, I know,' he said, as though he were speaking to a child,
and she knew that he did know, and that it would always be
this way with her, falling in love with the wrong man or the
man she could not have, exactly as though each time she did
it coldly and deliberately.

'Go on, Ned! Go home!' she said, and he understood that
too. It was better for him to go now, for otherwise it would
only mean the same old remorse and guilt for her. She tried
to smile at him from the door, and then went back quickly
and poured herself another drink. Then she opened the
living-room window and stood, looking out at the country
road, the bogs and the fields, now vague shapes in the darkness. At the end of the garden she seemed to see the poor
simpleton, staring at her, crushing a pair of her pants in his
hands and muttering, 'I love you.' She rested her hands on
the window-sill and leaned out as though she could see
him.

'Are you there?' she called.

There was no reply, only the whisper that always ran
over the dark uplands at night, and she raised her voice.

'Come in, whoever you are!' she said. 'There's nobody
here at all. The guards are gone. You're perfectly safe.'

For some reason she was convinced that he was there,
listening to her but paralysed, trapped in the snare of his
own crazy character even more than she was in hers. And
yet all she wanted was to come to terms with him, to lure
him out of himself and make him realize that there was a
world of warmth and friendship in which he could exist.
Then she slammed the window and gave way to an agony of
hopelessness. When people had mocked and criticized her
she had been afraid, but she had not given in, but now she
was really afraid because what she had to deal with was a
loneliness deeper than her own.

She knew now that Ned was right and that she no longer had a place of refuge from the outside world. She would never be able to live alone again; never again would she have a life of her own.

(1965)

THE IMPOSSIBLE MARRIAGE

IT wasn't till he was nearly thirty that Jim Grahame realized the trick that life had played on him. Up to that time he had lived very much like any other young man, with no great notion that he was being imposed upon. His father had died ten years before. Jim, an accountant in a provision store, had continued to accept his father's responsibilities, and his mother, a lively, sweet-natured little woman, had kept house for him in the way that only mothers can. They lived on in the house into which she had married; a big, roomy, awkward house on the edge of the country where the rent they paid was barely enough to keep the building in repair. Jim had never been very shy with girls, but none of them he had met seemed to him to be half the woman his mother was, and, unknown to himself, he was turning into a typical comfortable old bachelor who might or might not at the age of forty-five decide to establish a family of his own. His mother spoiled him, of course, and, in the way of only children, he had a troubled conscience because of the way he took advantage of it. But spoiling is a burden that the majority of men can carry a great deal of without undue hardship.

Then, by the seaside in Crosshaven, one Sunday, he went for a walk with a girl called Eileen Clery, who lived in the same quarter of Cork as himself, though he had never noticed her before. She wasn't the sort of girl who thrusts herself on people's attention, though she was good-looking enough, with a thin face that lit up beautifully when she smiled, and pale hair with gold lights in it. He tried to flirt with her, and was surprised and a little offended by her quick, almost violent, withdrawal. He had not mistaken her for a flighty type, but neither had he expected to meet an untouchable.

The curious thing was that she seemed to like him, and even arranged to meet him again. This time they sat in a nook on the cliffs, and Jim became more pressing. To his astonishment, she began to cry. He was exasperated, but he pretended a solicitude he did not altogether feel, and when she saw him apparently distressed, she sat up and smiled, though her tears still continued to flow freely. 'It's not that I wouldn't like it, Jim,' she said, drying her eyes and blowing her nose into a ridiculous little scrap of a handkerchief, 'only I don't like thinking about it.'

'Why on earth not, Eileen?' he asked with some amusement.

'Well, you see, I'm an only child, and I have my mother to look after,' she said, still sniffing.

'And I'm an only child, and I have a mother to look after,' Jim replied triumphantly, and then laughed outright at the absurdity of the coincidence. 'We're a pair,' he added with a rueful chuckle.

'Yes, aren't we?' Eileen said, laughing and sobbing at once, and then she rested her head on his chest, and made no further difficulties about his love-making.

Now, all books on the subject describe attraction in similar terms; tanned chests and voluptuous contours which really have very little to do with the matter. But what they rarely mention, the most powerful of all, is human loneliness. This is something that women face earlier than men, and Eileen had already faced it. Jim, though he had not faced it in the same way, was perceptive enough to see it reaching out before him, and up there on the cliffs overlooking Cork Harbour, watching a score of little sailing boats headed for Currabinny, they realized that they were in love, and all the more in love because their position was so obviously hopeless.

After that, they met regularly every week in Cork, to walk, or go to the pictures when it rained. They did it in the way of only children, taking precautions that became something of a joke to those who knew them. One evening, a girl crossing the New Bridge saw Jim Grahame standing there, and when she came to the second bridge was amused to see Eileen. 'Excuse my interfering, Miss Clery,' she said, 'but if it's Mr Grahame you're waiting for, he's waiting for you at the other bridge.' Eileen didn't know where to look; she blushed, she laughed, and finally joined her hands and said, 'Oh, thank you, thank you,' and ran like the wind.

It was like them to meet that way, miles from home, because they were pursued by the sense of guilt. They felt more pity for their mothers than for themselves and did their best to hide their dreadful secret out of some instinctive understanding of the fear of loneliness and old age that besets women whose families have grown and whose husbands are dead. Perhaps they even understood it too well, and apprehended more of it than was really there.

Mrs Grahame, whose intelligence service was better than Mrs Clery's, was the first to speak of the matter to them.

'I hear you're great friends with a girl called Clery from the Cross,' she said one evening in a tone of modest complaint. Jim was shaving by the back door. He started and turned to her with a look of amusement, but she was absorbed in her knitting, as always when she did not wish to look him in the face.

'Go on!' he said. 'Who told you that?'

'Why wouldn't I hear it when the whole road knows it?' she replied, avoiding his question. She liked her little mysteries. 'Wouldn't you bring her up some night?'

'You wouldn't mind?'

'Why would I mind, child? Little enough company we see.'

This was another of her favourite myths; that she never saw or spoke to anyone, though Jim could do little or nothing that she didn't hear about sooner or later.

One evening he brought Eileen home for tea, and though she was nervous and giggly, he could see that his mother took to her at once. Mrs Grahame worshipped her son, but she had always wished for a daughter, someone she could talk to as she could not talk to a man. Later in the evening, Eileen, realizing that she really was welcome, began to relax, and she and his mother exchanged the sort of gossip they both loved.

'Ah, Dinny Murphy was a bad head to her,' his mother would say darkly, referring to some object of charity in the neighbourhood.

'No, no, no, Mrs Grahame,' Eileen would say hastily, in her eagerness laying her hand on Mrs Grahame's arm. 'Poor Dinny wasn't the worst.'

'Look at that now!' Mrs Grahame would cry, putting down her knitting to fix Eileen with eyes that were bleak with tragedy. 'And the things they said about him! Eileen, haven't people *bad* tongues?'

'No, he wasn't, he wasn't,' Eileen would repeat, shaking her head. 'He took a drop, of course, but which of them doesn't, would you tell me?'

And Jim, who said nothing, smiled as he noticed how the voice of Eileen, young, eager, and intelligent, blended with his mother's in a perfect harmony of gossip. Mrs Grahame did not let her go without hinting delicately at her lost and lonely condition that made it impossible for her to know the truth about anything, and made her promise to come again. She became accustomed to Eileen's visits, and was quite hurt if a week went by without one. She even said with great resignation that of course she was no company for a lively young girl like that.

Then it was Mrs Clery's turn. She might hear of Eileen's visits to the Grahames, and be upset, but, on the other hand, she might be equally upset by an unexpected visit. So Eileen had to prepare her by telling her first how Jim was situated with regard to his own mother so that she wouldn't think he came to the house with any designs on Eileen. All they had to live on was Eileen's earnings and a few shillings pension which her mother drew.

They lived in a tiny cottage in a terrace off the road, with a parlour, a kitchen that they used as a living room, and two attic bedrooms upstairs. Mrs Clery was a shrewd old lady with a battered humorous face. She suffered from a variety of ailments, and, being slightly deaf, complained of them at great length in a loud, hectoring tone. She would put a firm hand on her interlocutor's knee while she talked, to make sure he didn't escape, and then stare blankly at the fireplace in concentration.

'So then, Jim, I had this second pain I was telling you about, and I had Dr O'Mahoney to the house, and he said – what did Dr O'Mahoney say about the second pain, Eileen?'

'He said you were an old humbug,' bawled Eileen.

'Dr O'Mahoney?' her mother said in wonderment. 'He did not. Ah, you divil you!'

At home, Eileen talked nervously, at the top of her voice, interrupting, contradicting, and bantering her mother till the old woman's face wrinkled up with glee and she blinked at Jim and groaned: 'Didn't I say she was a divil, Jim? Did you ever hear a girl talk to her mother that way? I'll engage you don't talk like that to your own poor mother.'

'His mother isn't always grousing,' Eileen yelled blithely from the backyard.

'Grousing? Who's grousing?' asked Mrs Clery, her eyes half closing with pleasure, like a cat's when you stroke it. 'Oh, my, I live in terror of her, Jim, boy, you never heard such a tongue! And the lies she tells! Me grousing!'

All the same it was pleasant for Jim and Eileen to have a place to turn to on a wet night when they didn't want to go to the pictures. Mostly, they went to Jim's. Mrs Grahame was more jealous than Eileen's mother. Even a hint of slight on the part of either of them would reduce her to mutinous tears, but if they sat with her for half an hour, she would get up and tiptoe gently out of the room as though she thought they were asleep. Her jealousy was only the measure of her generosity.

'Wisha, Jim,' she said roguishly one evening, putting down her knitting, 'wouldn't you and Eileen make a match of it?'

'A match?' Jim repeated mockingly, looking up from his book. 'I suppose you want to get rid of me?'

His mother could usually be diverted from any subject by teasing because she took everything literally even if she rarely took it far.

'Indeed, what a thing I'd do!' she said in a huff and went on with her knitting, full of childish rage at his reception of her generous proposal. But, of course, it didn't last. Ten minutes later, having forgotten her huff, she added, this time as though speaking to herself: 'Why, then, you wouldn't find many like her.'

'And where would we live?' he asked with gentle irony.

'My goodness, haven't ye the house?' she said, looking at him severely over her glasses. 'You don't think I'd stop to be in your way?'

'Oh, so you'd go to the workhouse and let Mrs Clery come here?'

'Wisha, aren't things very peculiar?' she said vaguely, and he knew that she was brooding on the coincidence by which he and Eileen had been drawn together. His mother and he were both familiar with the situation in its simple form, common as it is in Ireland, and could have listed a score of families where a young man or woman 'walked out' for years before he or she was in a position to marry, too often only to find themselves too old or tired for it.

'We're not thinking in that direction at all, Mrs Grahame, thank you all the same,' he said, giving her a sweet smile. 'It's got to be a double murder or nothing at all.'

He knew that in spite of her jealousy, Mrs Grahame resented this fate for them, but Mrs Clery jovially pretended that they should be grateful for their good fortune.

'Ye don't know how well off ye are,' she said. 'Ye're

young and healthy; a lot ye have to complain of. The way they rush into marriage you'd think they were robbing a bank. Soon enough they get tired of it, and then, oh, my! nothing is bad enough for them to say about one another.'

'So you don't approve of marriage, Mammy?' Eileen would ask demurely.

'Who said I don't approve of marriage?' her mother asked suspiciously, certain that the 'divils' were trapping her again. 'What matter whether you approve of it or not? That doesn't make it any better. Let ye be young while ye can, Jim,' she counselled, laying a rocky hand on Jim's knee. 'Ye'll be married long enough.'

But, of course, Eileen and himself did not share her views. On their evening walks they usually passed through one of the new developments, glanced into half-built houses with the enthusiasm of the children who played Cowboys and Indians in them; chatted with young husbands digging in little patches of garden that were mainly builders' rubble, and let themselves be invited in for cups of tea by young couples in all the pride and joy of recent possession. They saw nothing of the ugliness of it. They saw only the newness of everything as though it were life itself renewed; the way the evening sunlight brought up the freshness of the paint, the whiteness of the curtains, the tender green of the new grass. Later in the evening Eileen would say, shaking her head: 'I didn't think the curtains were right in the big corner windows, Jim, did you?' and Jim would know she had furnished the house in her own mind.

That year Jim suggested that he and Eileen should take their holidays together. This didn't suit Mrs Clery at all. She was sure it would give Eileen a bad name. Mrs Clery was all for their being young while they could, but only as long as they were being young under her eye. Jim knew it wasn't Eileen's good name that her mother worried about at all, but the possibility that their holiday might start something she could not control. He had his way; they went to a seaside place north of Dublin, and walked and swam and sunbathed to their hearts' content for a fortnight, going into the city when it rained.

On their way home, looking out at the Galtee mountains from the window of their carriage, he said: 'Next time we go on holidays like that, we should be married. It's not the same thing.'

'No, Jim, it isn't,' she agreed. 'But what can we do?'

'What's to stop us getting married?' he asked with a smile.

'Now?' she asked in alarm. 'But what would we do with our mothers?'

'What we do with them now,' he said with a shrug.

'You mean get married and go on the way we're going?'

'Why not? Of course, it's not what we want, but it's better than nothing.'

'But suppose – well, Jim, you know yourself there might be children.'

'I should hope so,' he replied. 'We can cross that bridge when we come to it. But anyhow, there's no particular reason we should have kids yet.'

'But Jim,' she asked timidly, 'wouldn't people talk?'

'Do you think they don't talk now?'

Jim was like that, and what Jim thought his mother would think, regardless of public opinion. She, of course, had seen nothing wrong with their going on holidays together, and Eileen, who had felt rather doubtful of it herself, now knew that she was right. She felt he was probably right now too, but she wasn't sure.

The more she thought of it, the more she felt he was, though her reasons were of a different kind. Jim didn't want to wait; he didn't want to grow old and sour in expectation of the day when they could get married; he wanted something, however little it might be, of the pleasure of marriage while they were still young enough to enjoy it. Eileen thought of it in a more mystical way, as a sort of betrothal which would bind them to one another, whatever life might have in store for them. She knew it was too much to hope that she and Jim would both be set free at the same time; one would be bound to be free long before the other, and then the real temptation would begin.

But she knew that even this she would not get without a fight with her mother. Mrs Clery was conventional to the heart, and besides she knew what happened in marriage. Eileen was very sweet and gentle now, but Eileen as wife or mother would be an altogether different proposition and one an old lady might be unable to handle at all.

'What a thing you'd do!' Mrs Clery gasped with one hand on her hip. 'What sort of marriage would that be? Him living there and you living here! You'd have the whole town laughing at you.'

'I don't really see what they'd have to laugh at, Mammy,' Eileen said earnestly. 'Any more than they have now.'

'Go off with him!' her mother said brokenly. 'Go off with him! I'd sooner go to the workhouse than be disgraced by ye.'

'But, Mammy,' persisted Eileen, laughing in spite of herself, 'we won't do anything to disgrace you, and you won't have to go to the workhouse or anywhere else.'

Mrs Grahame was upset too, but it was her pride that was hurt. What the neighbours would say did not worry her at all, but it seemed to her that it was her dependence on Jim that forced him into this caricature of a marriage. If by getting out of his way she could have made it easier for him, she would cheerfully have gone into the workhouse. But when Jim explained that even if he agreed to her doing so, it would change nothing regarding Eileen and her mother, she saw that he was right. When next Eileen called, Mrs Grahame embraced her and muttered: 'Ye poor children! Ye poor, distracted children!'

'You don't think we're doing wrong, Mrs Grahame?' Eileen asked, beginning to be tearful herself.

'Sure, how could you be doing wrong, child?' Mrs Grahame exclaimed angrily. 'Why would ye care what anybody thinks? People who never sacrificed a thing in their lives!'

Then Mrs Clery threw a fit of the sulks, would not speak to Jim when he called, and finally refused to attend what she called 'the mock wedding'. Mrs Clery had little experience of that sort of thing, but she did know when she had been tricked, and she had been tricked by Jim. He had come to the house as a friend and stolen her only daughter from under her eyes. As for all this talk of putting her first, she didn't believe a word of it. A man who would do what he had done would think nothing of putting arsenic in her cup of tea.

Before she left for the church that morning, Eileen went in to her mother and asked gently: 'Mammy, won't you even wish me luck?' But all her mother said was 'Go away, you bold thing!'

'I'll be back tomorrow night in time to get your supper, Mammy,' Eileen said meekly.

'You needn't come back at all,' said her mother.

Eileen was very upset, but Mrs Grahame only scoffed at it when they said goodbye outside the church.

'Ah, she'll get over it, child,' she said. 'Old people are all lick alike. I'm the same myself, if the truth was known. I'll see her on the way home and give her a bit of my mind.'

'And, Mrs Grahame, if you wouldn't mind making her an egg flip, she'd be easier to talk to,' Eileen said earnestly. 'She's very fond of egg flips, and she likes a lot of whiskey in them.'

'I'll give her an egg flip,' said Mrs Grahame, suddenly lighthearted because her own savage jealousy melted in the thought of comforting another old woman in her tantrums. She had a job on her hands, even with the egg flip.

'Don't talk to me, ma'am!' cried Mrs Clery. 'Young people today are all the same; all selfish, all for pleasure.'

'How can you say it, Mrs Clery?' Mrs Grahame asked indignantly. 'There isn't a better daughter in Ireland. I'd be the last to criticize Jim, but I only wish I had one like her.'

'And when the children start coming?' asked Mrs Clery, looking at her as if she were out of her mind.

'You reared one yourself.'

' 'Tisn't alike, ma'am,' said Mrs Clery and refused to be comforted. She was intelligent enough to realize that the presence of another baby in the house might rob her of some of the attention to which she felt entitled, and might even result in her being totally deprived of her privileges. Young people today were so selfish!

After their one-day honeymoon, Jim and Eileen obediently returned to their duties as though they had never been married at all. Yet Eileen, when you met her on the road, was exceedingly lighthearted and lightheaded, sporting her ring like any young bride. She needed all the joy her new position gave her because her mother had been shrewd enough in her summing up of what the neighbours' attitude would be. The marriage had become a matter of scandalous jokes, and remained so as long as it lasted. Even from intimate friends, Eileen got little jabs that reminded her of her anomalous wifehood. It wasn't that the neighbours were uncharitable, but their feelings about marriage, like their feelings about death, had a certain fierceness that was obvious even in their dislike of second marriages. This marriage that seemed to end at the church door was a mockery of all they believed in, so they took their revenge as people will whose dearest beliefs have been slighted.

Jim affected not to notice the scandal. He had his mother's curious imperviousness to public opinion, and he dropped in on Eileen as though nothing in particular could be said against him. Eileen dropped in rather more frequently on him and his mother, and Jim and she went off for a fortnight in the summer to Kerry or Connemara. It took Mrs Clery a full year to get used to it, and all that time she watched Eileen closely, expecting her each week to show signs of pregnancy. Perhaps it was fortunate that there were none. Heaven alone knows what she might have done.

Then Mrs Grahame fell ill, and Jim nursed her by day

while Eileen took over from him at night. She was dying, and in the intervals of consciousness, she moulded Eileen's hands with her own and said: 'I always wanted a daughter, and I had my wish. I had my wish. Ye'll be happy now that ye have the house to yerselves. You'll look after Jim for me?'

'I'll look after him for you,' Eileen said, and on the night when his mother died she let him sleep on.

'I thought I'd better not wake you, Jim,' she said when she roused him next morning. 'You were so tired and Mammy went so peacefully ... That's the way she'd have wished it, Jim,' she added gravely when she saw his look of surprise.

'I dare say you're right, Eileen,' he agreed.

But their troubles were far from being at an end. When they proposed to shift into Jim's house, Mrs Clery raised more of a hullaballoo than she had raised over the marriage.

'Is it up among strangers?' she cried aghast.

'Strangers half a mile away, Mammy?' Eileen exclaimed, still unable to conceal a laugh at her mother's extraordinary reception of every new proposal.

'Half a mile?' her mother echoed dully. ' 'Tis a mile.'

'And you think your old friends would desert you?' asked Eileen.

'I wouldn't ask them,' her mother replied with dignity. 'I couldn't sleep in a place where I wouldn't hear the sound of the trams. Jim's mother died in her own house. Oh, my, isn't it a queer thing he wouldn't let me die in mine!'

And once more Jim and Eileen had to resign themselves to frustration. They could offer no adequate substitute for the soothing squeak of the trams climbing Summerhill from the city, and as Eileen saw, it would be folly for them to give up Jim's excellent house, which they would need later on, and come to share her own tiny cottage with a cranky mother-in-law.

Instead, they played at being married. On a couple of evenings each week, Eileen would give her mother supper early.

and then come to Jim's house and have supper ready for him when he got in from the shop. When she heard his key in the lock, she ran to the front door to meet him in her white housecoat, and he would let on to be suitably astonished at seeing her. As they went in, she would point silently to the big fire she had lit in the living-room, and they would have supper together and read or talk till he saw her home coming on to midnight. Yet, even with the extra work, it gave them both a deep pleasure to make the big bed that Eileen never slept in except as a visitor, to wash up together, or, best of all, to entertain some friends, just as though Eileen did not, like Cinderella, have to fly back at midnight to her old part as daughter and nurse. Some day, they felt, the house would really be theirs, and she would open the door in the morning to milkman and breadman.

But this was not how things happened. Instead, Jim fell seriously ill, and rather than consent to the conflict which he knew this would set up in Eileen's mind between her duty to him and her duty to her mother, he chose to go to hospital. Two years after his mother's death, he died there.

Something seemed to happen to Eileen at this point that made even her mother afraid. There was no argument between them as to what she should do. She shut up her own cottage, and her mother joined her in Jim's house where she received his relatives. The body had been taken to the church, and when Jim's family came, Eileen had lunch ready for them, and chatted as she served, as though the trouble had been theirs rather than hers. It was a cold lunch, and she was full of apologies. At the graveside while they wept, she showed no sign of tears. When the grave had been covered over Jim and his mother, she stood there silently, her head bowed, and Jim's aunt, an enormous woman, came up and took her two hands.

'You're a great little girl,' she whispered huskily. ''Twon't be forgotten for you.'

'But, Auntie,' Eileen replied, 'that's the way Jim would have liked it. It makes me feel close to him, and it won't be long till we're together again. Once Mammy goes, there'll be nothing to keep me.'

There was something about her words, and her dry-eyed air and her still-youthful face that the other woman found disconcerting.

'Ah, nonsense, child!' she said lightly. 'We all feel that way. You'll be happy yet, and you'll deserve it. One of these days you'll have a houseful of your own.'

'Oh, no, Auntie,' Eileen replied with a sweet smile that was curiously knowledgeable and even condescending, as though Jim's aunt were too much of a child to understand. 'You know yourself I could never find another husband like Jim. People can't be as happy as that a second time, you know. That would be too much to ask.'

And relatives and even neighbours began to realize that Eileen was only telling the truth; that in spite of everything she had been intensely happy, happy in some way they could not understand, and that what had seemed to them a mockery of marriage had indeed been one so complete and satisfying that beside it, even by their standards, a woman might think everything else in the world a mere shadow.

(1957)

UNAPPROVED ROUTE

BETWEEN men and women, as between neighbouring states, there are approved roads which visitors must take. Others they take at their peril, no matter how high-minded their intentions may be.

When I lived in England I became friendly with another Irishman, named Frankie Daly. Frankie was the sort of man men like. He was scrupulous, but not so as to irritate people who might have scruples of a different kind. Exacting with himself, he was tolerant of others. The good qualities he had – conscientiousness, loyalty, and generosity – were not those he demanded of his friends, and, as a result, they made great efforts to show them where he was concerned. Even Mick Flynn, who lived by borrowing, made a hullabaloo about paying back a pound he owed to Frankie.

Frankie and I were also friendly with two school-mistresses who had a little cottage in School Lane, and they frequently joined us in the pub for a drink. Rosalind and Kate could have been sisters, they had so little in common. Kate was a born spinster, lean, plain, and mournful, and with the kindest heart in the world. She was very left-wing and tended to blame most of her troubles on capitalism. Rosalind was a good-looking girl with a fat and rather sullen face who was always up and down with some man, usually – according to Kate, at any rate – of the shadiest kind. Women with a man on their hands usually vote Tory – they dislike being interrupted – and Rosalind was a Conservative. Cooking being a form of activity associated with love-making, she was also an excellent cook, while Kate, who adored food, not only couldn't cook herself, but was driven into hysterics of fastidiousness by the mere sight of cooking fat. She felt about grease as she felt about men, and I sometimes had a suspicion that she identified the two. I often wondered how she could face the liquidation of capitalists and all the blood and mess it would involve.

One day another fellow countryman of Frankie and myself turned up on a temporary job. He was a shambling, good-natured, high-spirited man, given to funny stories and inexplicable fits of morose anger. Lodgings were scarce and hotels expensive, so the girls offered him a room in the cottage. He settled down so well with them that inside a week or so he and Rosalind were lovers. She simply could not be kept away from men.

Kate then devoted herself entirely to the task of hating Jim Hourigan, and being as rude to him as she dared with Rosalind there. Having a lover of Rosalind's in the cottage was like having endless greasy frying-pans to dodge; she couldn't move without seeing a masculine singlet or a pair of socks. Kate derived enormous pleasure from her own griefs, and she told us with gloomy humour that it had been bad enough before, lying awake and wondering what Rosalind was up to, but this had been nothing to lying awake and knowing what she was up to. She couldn't kick up a row with Rosalind, who had an unpredictable and violent temper where men were concerned. Kate rationalized this to herself by saying that Rosalind, being a girl of exceptional intelligence, knew they were all wasters, but was too proud to admit it. She told us that Rosalind never had had any taste, that all the men she knew had exploited her, that Jim Hourigan was only another of them, and that the only consolation was that she was there herself, ready to pick up the pieces when the inevitable disillusionment came. Frankie and I only laughed at Kate's groans. We didn't know what sort Jim Hourigan was, and we didn't really care much.

When his job ended, he returned to Ireland, after making many promises of bringing the girls for a long summer holiday there, and of returning himself at the first opportunity. Kate was very cheerful because she was quite convinced that he didn't mean a word of it – she had the lowest view of his character and motives – and was delighted to have Rosalind and the cottage to herself again. Rosalind, too, was cheerful because, never before having had anything to do with an Irishman, she took all his promises for Gospel, had everything ready for her holiday in the summer, and was certain that Hourigan would then ask her to marry him. She wrote him long, animated letters, cleverly recalling our little town and the characters he had met there, and quoting Kate's doleful predictions about the weather, the European situation, and the cost of living.

There was an alarming lack of response to her letters; finally they did produce a wet spark of a picture postcard, saying how much Hourigan looked forward to coming back, that might have encouraged a more persevering correspondent, but merely infuriated Rosalind. She wasn't accustomed to having her brilliant letters treated with such lack of ceremony and told him so, but this didn't produce even a spark. Kate began to put on weight, though how she did was a miracle, because Rosalind was so upset she refused to cook, and Kate had not only to eat sausages – which she loathed – but even to clean the disgusting frying-pan herself.

But that wasn't the end of Kate's troubles. Imprudent as usual, Rosalind was having a baby. Now, in the natural way of things, a nice baby without any messy father to get in the way would have been Kate's idea of bliss, but bliss of that sort is not contemplated in English provincial towns. To begin with, Rosalind would lose her job; women teachers cannot have babies without marriage lines; the thing is unknown. Besides, the landlady would be bound to ask them to leave; this was also part of the drill, and even if the landlady had been a considerate woman, which she wasn't, she would still have found it difficult to overlook such conduct. They would have to try and hush things up, and put the baby out to nurse.

This was where Rosalind became completely un-manageable. She said she wanted to keep her baby, and she didn't mind who knew. Just the same she stopped coming to the public-house with the rest of us, and Kate, gloomier than ever, came alone. She was depressed by her failure to make Rosalind see reason. It would only be for a couple of years, and then they could make some arrangement, like pre-tending to adopt the baby.

'That wouldn't be so very good, Kate,' Frankie said when she mentioned it to him.

'Well, what else can she do, Frankie? Go out as a char-woman?'

'Those are questions that answer themselves, Kate,' he said stubbornly. 'A baby put out to nurse is a question that never answers itself.'

Next evening, without saying anything to Kate or me, he called to the cottage and found Rosalind sitting alone over the fire.

'Coming down to the pub, Rosa?' he asked cheerfully.

'No, Frankie, thanks,' she said, without looking up.

'Why not? You know it's not the same without you.'

She covered her face with her hands. Frankie sat awk-wardly with his legs stretched out, sucking his pipe.

'Kate tells me you don't want to part with the child.'

'It seems I'm not likely to be asked.'

'All the same, I think you're right and Kate is wrong,' he said gravely.

'That's easily said, Frankie,' she replied. 'It isn't so easy for Kate, with her job to mind.'

'If that's how you feel about it, wouldn't it be better for you to marry?'

'The man who got me would get a treasure,' she said savagely. 'Whistled after in the street!'

'That's a matter for him,' said Frankie. 'Plenty of men would be very glad to marry you. You mustn't let a thing like this make you undervalue yourself.'

'Ah, talk sense, Frankie!' she said wearily. 'Who'd marry me in the middle of all this scandal?'

'I would, to begin with – if you hadn't anyone you liked better.'

'You?' she asked incredulously.

'And consider myself very much honoured,' Frankie added steadily.

'Are you serious, Frankie?' she asked, almost angrily.

'Of course I'm serious.'

'And face all the humiliation of it?'

'There isn't any humiliation,' he said flatly. 'That's where you're mistaken. There's no humiliation where there hasn't been any offence. The offence is in deceiving others, not in being deceived ourselves.'

'Oh, I can't, Frankie, I can't,' she said desperately. 'I've made a fool of myself over this waster, and I can't let another man shoulder my burdens.'

'There's no particular burden either,' he said. 'You mustn't think I'm asking you only because you're in a fix. I'd have asked you anyway when this thing was all over and you could make up your own mind. I'm only asking now in case it might make the immediate future a bit easier.'

'Why didn't you ask me before?'

'Maybe because I felt I hadn't much to offer you,' Frankie said, with a shy smile.

'My God,' she said, rising. 'I'd have married you like a shot.'

She sat on his knee and hugged him despairingly. He was a clumsy lover. He talked in an apologetic, worried tone about his job, his home, and his family; how much he earned and where they could live. She didn't listen. She thought of what it would mean to her to start life again, free of this nightmare. Then she took him by the shoulders and looked into his eyes with the air of a sleepwalker.

'I'll do it,' she said. 'God help me, Frankie, I hate it, but I'll do it for the kid's sake. All I can say is that I'll make it up to you. You needn't be afraid of that. I'll make it up to you all right.'

Kate, whose low view of life had led her to take a low view of its Creator, almost got converted because of it. She had always liked Frankie, but her experience of people she liked had been that they only got her into fresh trouble, and that it was better, if you could manage it, to have nothing to do with anybody. She wasn't the only one who admired Frankie's behaviour. It dawned on others of us that he had done exactly what we would have done ourselves except for what people might think. Actually, as we discovered, 'people', meaning the neighbours with one or two exceptions, liked Rosalind and were pleased to see her escape the machine of social ignominy reserved for women with more feeling than calculation in them.

Frankie and Rosalind were married quietly and went to live in a little cottage some miles outside the town, a rather lonely cottage with low beams, high chimneys, and breakneck staircases, but it had a big garden which Rosalind enjoyed. She kept on her job; she knew the other teachers knew, but now it only amused her. It was wonderful to have Frankie there as a prop. Up to this, all the men she had lived with had taken advantage of her, and she had accepted it in a cynical, good-humoured way, as part of the price you had to pay for being too fond of them. She believed, as Kate did, that men were like that, but she was lacking in any desire to reform them.

Under Frankie's care she grew round as a tum, stupid, and quite remarkably beautiful, while Kate managed to look as like the anxious father of her unborn child as a girl could look. But the change in Frankie was even more remarkable. He had always kept a youthful freshness, but now he suddenly began to look like a boy of seventeen. It might have been something to do with Rosalind's cooking – Kate, who had begun to feel the lack of it, visited them every day – but he rang her up regularly at school to see that she was all right, raced for his bus to get home early in the evenings, and took her for her evening walk to the pub. He was full of banter and tricks, and Rosalind looked on with the affectionate calm of a woman watching the man she loves make a fool of himself. And it really was pleasant those summer evenings outside the public-house, watching that late flowering of emotion, the bachelor crust of caution breaking up, the little shoots of sentiment beginning to peer out.

Their happiness was lyrical. It was only at odd times that Rosalind remembered her griefs, and usually it was in the early morning when she was waked by the heaving of the child within her, listened to the birds outside their window, and felt deserted even with Frankie beside her. Not to wake him, she sniffled quietly into her handkerchief, her back turned on him and her body shaken with suppressed sobs. When he woke, she still tried to keep away from him.

'What ails you now didn't ail you before?' he would ask humorously.

'What you've got in me.'

'What's that?'

'I told you – a daisy!'

'No, that was what I told you,' he said, and slapped her bottom affectionately.

Then she bawled without restraint and beat her stomach.

'Why can't it be yours?' she cried despairingly.

'One thing at a time,' said Frankie.

He believed her; that was his mistake. He really thought when he heard her lonely weeping that it was merely the ambiguity of her position that caused it, and not the humiliation of being rejected and hounded into marriage with someone else by a tramp like Hourigan. Frankie was a decent man; he didn't realize that in circumstances like those no woman can ever be happy, even with the best man in the world – even with the man she loves. Love, in fact, has nothing to do with it. To ignore that is to ignore a woman's vanity, the mainspring of her character.

Her time came in the middle of the night, and Frankie returned from the nursing home in the early morning in a stupor of misery and astonishment; misery at the mere possibility that her life might be in danger, astonishment that anyone's life could possibly mean so much to him. He lit the fire, but then found that he couldn't bear the little cottage without her; it too seemed in a stupor of misery, wondering when she would come back, put on that housecoat, boil that kettle, and wash those dishes. He wanted to make himself breakfast, but could not bring himself to touch the things that were properly hers and that stood waiting for her with the infinite patience of inanimate things. He swore at himself when he realized that he was identifying his grief with that of a common tea-kettle. He had some breakfast in a café, and then went off, walking through the countryside, merely halting for a drink while he rang up the nursing home. It was evening before everything was over and Rosalind and the child – a son – safe, and then he took a car straight there.

She was still stupefied with drugs when he was admitted, but she clung to him passionately.

'Don't look!' she said fiercely. 'Not till the next time.'

'I thought he was yours,' Frankie said with a grin and smiled down at the little morsel in the cot. 'Cripes!' he added savagely. 'Wouldn't you think they could get them out without clawing them?'

'Did you hear the children playing on the doorstep?' she asked happily.

'No,' Frankie said in surprise. 'What were they playing?'

'*Hamlet*, I think,' she said closing her eyes, and, seeing how her thoughts drifted in and out of the drug, he tiptoed out. In sheer relief he knocked back three whiskeys in quick succession, but failed to get drunk. Then he tried for some of the old gang to sit and drink with, but, by one of those coincidences that always occur at moments like that, we were all out. It was just that he didn't want to go home. When he did get out of the bus and crossed the common towards the cottage he saw a man's figure step out of the shadow of the trees beside it and knew at once who it was. His heart sank.

'Frankie!' Jim Hourigan said imploringly, 'I'd like a word with you.'

Frankie halted. He had a sudden feeling of foreboding.

'You'd better come inside,' he said in a troubled voice.

He went ahead into the sitting-room and switched on the light, and the electric fire which stood in the big open hearth. Then he turned and faced Hourigan, who was standing by the door. The man looked half distracted, his eyes were wild, his hair was in disorder.

'What is it?' he asked curtly.

'Frankie,' Hourigan muttered. 'I want a word with Rosalind.'

'Rosalind is in hospital.'

'I know, I know,' Hourigan said, flapping his hands like an old man. 'She said she was going there. But I wanted to see you first, to get your permission. It's only to explain to her, Frankie – that's all.'

Frankie concealed his surprise at Hourigan's statement that Rosalind had told him anything.

'I don't think she's in a state of seeing anybody, you know,' he said in a level tone. 'The boy was born only a couple of hours ago.'

'Christ!' Hourigan said, beating the table with his fist and shaking his head as though tossing water from his eyes. 'That's all that was missing. I came late for the fair as usual. My first child is born and I'm not even there. All right, Frankie, all right,' he added in a crushed tone, 'I see 'tis no good. But tell her all the same. Tell her I never knew a thing about it till I got her letter. That God might strike me dead this minute if the idea ever crossed my mind!'

Frankie looked at him in surprise. There was no mistaking the man's abject misery.

'What letter was this?' he asked.

'The letter she sent me before she went in,' Hourigan hurried on, too distraught to notice the bewilderment in Frankie's voice. 'You don't think I'd have treated her like that if I knew? You can think what you like of me, Frankie, and it won't be anything worse than I think of myself, but not that, Frankie, not that! I wouldn't do it to a woman I picked up in the street, and I loved that girl, Frankie. I declare to God I did.' He began to wave his arms wildly again, looking round the little sitting-room without seeing anything. 'It's just that I'm no damn good at writing letters. The least thing puts me off. I'd be saying to myself I'd be there before the letter. I said the same thing to her on a card, Frankie, but then, the mother died, and I was in a terrible state – oh, the usual things! I know 'tis no excuse, and I'm not making excuses, but that's the way I am. If I had any idea I'd have been over to her by the first boat. You must tell her that, Frankie. She must know it herself.'

'When did you get this letter?' asked Frankie.

'Oh, only yesterday, Frankie,' exclaimed Hourigan, entirely missing the import of Frankie's question. 'I swear to God I didn't waste an hour. I'm travelling all night. I couldn't sleep and I couldn't eat. It was all that damn letter. It nearly drove me out of my mind. Did you see it, Frankie?'

'No,' said Frankie.

'Well, you'd better. Mind, I don't blame her a bit, but it's not true, it's not true!'

He took the letter from his wallet and passed it to Frankie. Frankie sat down and put on his glasses. Hourigan bent over the back of the armchair, reading it again in a mutter.

'Dear Jim Hourigan,' Frankie read silently. 'By this time tomorrow I'll be in a hospital, having your child. This will probably be more satisfaction to you than it is to me and my husband. I am sure you will be disappointed to know that I have a husband, but in this life we can't expect everything.'

'Now, that's what I mean, Frankie,' Hourigan said desperately, jabbing at the lines with his forefinger. 'That's not fair, and she knows it's not fair. She knows I'm not as mean as that, whatever faults I have.'

'I wouldn't worry too much about that,' Frankie said heavily, realizing that Hourigan and he were not reading the same letter. It was almost as though they were not concerned with the same woman. This was a woman whom Frankie had never seen. He went on reading.

'If the child takes after you, it might be better for more than Frank and myself that it shouldn't live. My only hope is that it may learn something from my husband. If ever a good man can make up to a child for the disaster of a bad father, your child will have every chance. So far as I can, I'll see that he gets it, and will never know any more of you than he knows now.' It was signed in full: 'Rosalind Daly'.

Hourigan sighed.

'You explain to her, Frankie,' he said despairingly. 'I couldn't.'

'I think it would be better if you explained it yourself,' Frankie said, folding up the letter and giving it back.

'You think she'll see me?' Hourigan asked doubtfully.

'I think she'd better see you,' Frankie said in a dead voice.

'Only for ten minutes, Frankie; you can tell her that. Once I explain to her, I'll go away, and I give you my word that neither of you will ever see me here again.'

'I'll talk to her myself in the morning,' Frankie said. 'You'd better ring me up at the office some time after twelve.'

Hourigan shambled away across the common, blabbing poetic blessings on Frankie's head and feeling almost elated. How Frankie felt, he never said. Perhaps if Hourigan had known how he felt, he might have left that night without seeing Rosalind. He wasn't a bad chap, Jim Hourigan, though not exactly perceptive, even as regards the mother of his child.

But Rosalind had perception enough for them both. When Frankie called next morning, the effect of the drug had worn off, and she knew from the moment he entered that something serious had happened. He was as gentle as ever, but he had withdrawn into himself, the old Frankie of the days before his marriage, hurt but self-sufficient. She grabbed his hands feverishly.

'Is anything wrong at home, Frankie?'

'Nothing,' he replied in embarrassment. 'Just a visitor, that's all.'

'A visitor? Who?'

'I think you know,' he said gently.

'What brought that bastard?' she hissed.

'Apparently a letter from you.'

Suddenly, she began to weep, the core of her hysteria touched.

'I didn't tell you because I didn't want to upset you,' she sobbed. 'I just wanted him to know how I despised him.'

'He seems to have got the idea,' Frankie said dryly. 'Now, he wants to see you, to explain.'

'Damn his explanations!' she cried hysterically. 'I know what you think – that I sent that letter without telling you so as to bring him here. How could I know there was enough manliness in him to make him even do that? Can't you imagine how I felt, Frankie?'

'You know,' he said paternally, 'I think you'd better have a word with him and make up your mind about exactly what you did feel.'

'Oh, Christ!' she said. 'I tell you I only meant to hurt him. I never meant to hurt you, and that's all I've succeeded in doing.'

'I'd rather you didn't let your feelings run away with you again and hurt yourself and the child,' Frankie said in a gentler tone.

'But how can I avoid hurting myself when I'm hurting you?' she asked wildly. 'Do you think this is how I intended to pay you back for what you did for me? Very well; if he's there, send him up and I'll tell him. I'll tell him in front of you. I'll tell you both exactly how I feel. Will that satisfy you?'

'He'll call this afternoon,' Frankie said firmly. 'You'd better see him alone. You'd better let him see the child alone. And remember,' he added apologetically, 'whatever you decide on, I agree to beforehand. I may have behaved selfishly before. I don't want to do it again.'

He smiled awkwardly and innocently, still bewildered by the disaster which had overtaken him, and Rosalind held her hands to her temples in a frenzy. She had never realized before how hurt he could be, and probably not even known that she might hurt him.

'I suppose you think I'm going to let you divorce me so that I can go back to Ireland with that waster? I'd sooner throw myself and the child into a pond. Oh, very well, I'll settle it, I'll settle it. Oh, God!' she said between her teeth. 'What sort of fool am I?'

And as he went down the stairs, Frankie knew that he was seeing her for the last time as his wife, and that, when they met again, she would be merely the mother of Jim Hourigan's child, and realized with a touch of bitterness that there are certain forms of magnanimity which are all very well between men, but are misplaced in dealing with women, not because they cannot admire them, but because they seem to them irrelevant to their own function in life. When he saw Hourigan again he knew that the change had already taken place. Though nothing had been decided, Jim Hourigan was almost professionally protective of Frankie's interests and feelings. That was where the iron in Frankie came out. He made it plain that his interests were not in question.

There were plenty – Kate among them – to say that he had behaved absurdly; that with a little more firmness on his part the crisis would never have arisen; that Rosalind was in no condition to make the decision he had forced on her and needed only gentle direction to go on as she had been going;

that, in fact, he might have spared her a great deal of un-happiness by refusing to see Jim Hourigan in the first place.

As for unhappiness, nothing I have heard suggests that Rosalind is unhappy with Jim Hourigan. It is a grave mistake to believe that that sort of thing leads to unhappiness. Frankie's conduct certainly does, but is that not because to people like him happiness is merely an incidental, something added, which taken away, leaves them no poorer than before?

(1952)

MUSIC WHEN SOFT VOICES DIE

DURING the lunch hour the male clerks usually went out, leaving myself and the three girls behind. While they ate their sandwiches and drank their tea, they chattered away, thirteen to the dozen. Half their conversation I didn't understand at all, and the other half bored me to tears. I usually drifted into the hallway with a Western. As a boy, I acted out whatever I was reading – taking steady aim, drawing rein, spurring to the rescue, and clutching at my shoulder where an Indian arrow had lodged – and the girls interrupted me with their comments.

They were nice girls, though. Joan, who was nineteen, was my favourite. She was masterful and warmhearted; she would take my part when I got in trouble, and whenever she saw me with the sign of tears, she would put her arm round me and say, 'Look, Larry – *you* tell Mr Scally if he says *another* word to you, I'll tear his *eyes* out.' She talked like that, all in italics. I liked Nora, too, but not so much. Sometimes she was very sweet and sometimes she didn't see you, and you never knew which it would be. Marie I didn't really like at all in those days. She was the prettiest of the three – thin, tall, and nunlike, with a queer stiff way of holding herself and an ironic intonation in her beautiful voice. Marie usually just didn't see you. I thought she was an old snob.

The three girls had fellows, and I knew these, too, mostly from seeing them hang about the office in the evening. Joan was going with a long-haired medical student called Mick Shea, with no hat and no religion, and she was always making novenas for his conversion. Nora went with a dressy fellow in Montenotte, the classy quarter of Cork, but she had a sort of underground understanding with a good-look-ing postman called Paddy Lacy, who used to stop me in the street and give me gallant messages for her. She never walked out with him that I knew of, but he was certain she loved him, and it shocked me that a superior fellow like a postman would not have more sense. Marie was going strong with a chap called Jim Holbrook, a rather snobbish intellectual type, who lived up my way.

Thirty years has turned the girls and myself into old friends. Only Nora is still at the office. Joan owns a private hotel, and Marie is the harassed mother of two wild children. She is still beautiful, sedate, and caustic. Not one word of their conversation ever seemed to register in my memory, which was full of valuable information about American states and Indian nations, wigwams, colts, derringers, and coyotes; yet now that I cannot remember anything of what I read, it seems to me that I can hear the girls as though they were in the same room with me, like the voices of Shelley's poem, trembling on the edge of pure music.

'Do you know, I have a *great* admiration for that girl?' Joan begins in her eager italics.

'Go on!' Nora says lightly. 'What did she do?'

'I admire her pluck, Nora,' Joan says, emphasizing three syllables out of seven. 'When I *think* what she went through!'

'Ah, for God's sake, what did she go through?' Nora asks sceptically.

'That's all you know, Nora,' Joan says in a blood curdling voice. 'You never had an illegitimate kid to support, and Susie had.'

'Good job, too,' Nora says. 'I can't support myself.'

'What did you say she had, Joan?' Marie asks incredu-lously.

'A kid.'

'Well!' Marie exclaims, looking brightly from one to the other. 'The friends some people have!'

'Oh, it's true, Marie.'

'That's what makes it so peculiar, Joan,' Marie says with a shrug.

'What did she do with it?' Nora asks inquisitively.

'I suppose I really shouldn't say it, Nora, but of course it's really no secret. With the way the police watch girls like that, everything leaks out eventually. She had to farm him out in Rochestown. He must be about twelve now.'

'And does he know who his mother is?' asks Nora.

'Not at all, girl,' says Joan. 'How could she tell him? I suppose she's never even seen him. Gosh, I'm sorry for that girl!'

'I'd be sorrier for the kid,' Nora says.

'Oh, I know, Nora, I know,' Joan says earnestly. 'But what could the poor girl do? I mean, what would *we* do if we were in her place?'

And now that the voices grow clearer in my mind, I realize that Joan is the leader of the trio. It is she who sets the tempo, and it is her violin that holds it all together. Marie, with her deep beautiful voice, is the viola; Nora, for all that her voice sounds thin and squeaky, is the cello.

'Honestly, Joan, the things you say!' Marie cries, but without indignation. Marie sometimes behaves as though Joan is not really right in the head, and manages to suggest that she herself alone, with her nunlike air and caustic tongue, represents normality.

But Joan, who believes that Marie cultivates a blind spot for anything it doesn't suit her to see, only smiles knowingly. 'Well, we're all human, girl,' she says.

'Ah, nonsense, Joan!' says Marie. 'There must be something wrong with a girl like that.'

'There's something wrong with every girl or else she'd be a man,' says Nora.

'Ah, with the best will in the world, girl, I couldn't imagine myself going on like that,' says Marie. 'I suppose I mustn't be human,' she adds with a shrug, meaning that if this is what it's like to be human, so much the worse for humanity. 'Of course,' she ends, to show she has feelings, like anyone else, 'we all like a bit of sport, but that's different.'

'Oh, but it's not different, Marie,' Joan says warmly, and again the fiddle proclaims the theme. 'That's where you make your big mistake. What you call "a bit of sport" is only a matter of degree. God knows, I'm not what you'd call a public menace, but if I didn't watch my step, I could very easily see it happening to me.'

'So could I,' Nora says, and then begins to blush. 'And I don't know what I'd do about it, either.'

'Well, what could you do?' asks Marie. 'Assuming that such a thing could happen, which is assuming quite a lot.'

'I suppose I'd have to go to England and have it there,' says Nora gloomily.

'England?' says Marie.

'That would be all right if you knew someone in England, Nora,' says Joan. 'I mean, someone you could rely on.'

' "All right"?' echoes Marie. 'I should think starting life again in a foreign country with a baby, like that, would hardly be described as "all right". Or maybe I'm lacking in initiative?'

'Well, it would either be that or make him marry you,' says Nora.

'I was wondering when you'd think of marriage,' says Marie.

'That mightn't be as easy as it sounds, either, Marie,' says Joan. 'I think Nora means the fellow wouldn't want to marry you.'

'Yes, and I think it's rotten!' says Nora. 'A fellow pretending to a girl that she's the only thing in the world he cares for, till she makes a fool of herself for him, and then he cuts his hook.'

'Well,' Joan says practically, 'I suppose we're all the same when we get what we want.'

'If that's all a man wants, couldn't somebody give it to him on a spoon?' says Nora.

'I'd simply say in a case like that that the man began to see what sort the girl was,' Marie says, having completely misunderstood Nora's remark.

'And what sort would you say *he* was?' Nora asks.

'Ah, well,' Marie replies comfortably, 'that's different, Nora. Considering the sort of sheltered lives women lead, it's up to them to set a standard. You can't expect the same sort of thing from men. Of course, I think he should be made to marry her.'

'But who'd make him, Marie?' asks Joan.

'Well, I suppose his family would, if it was for nothing but to avoid a scandal.'

'Ask any mother in Cork would she sooner a scandal or a daughter-in-law,' Nora says cynically.

'Then of course the priest would have to make him,' says Marie, still unperturbed.

'That's what I find so hard to imagine, though,' Joan says, and then her tone changes, and she becomes brilliant and mocking. 'I mean, it's all very well talking about it like this in the peace and quiet of the office, but imagine if I had to go up tonight after dark to the presbytery and talk to old Canon Cremin about it. "Excuse me, Canon, but I've been keeping company with a boy called Mick Shea, and it just so happens that he made a bit too free with me, and I was wondering would you ever mind running down and telling him to marry me." Cripes, if I was the Canon, I'd take my stick to a one like that!'

'Lovely marriage 'twould be anyway,' says Nora.

'Exactly, Nora,' Joan says, in her dramatic way, laying her hand on Nora's arm. 'That's just what I mean. How on earth could you spend the rest of your life with a man after having to do that to get him to marry you?'

'How he could spend the rest of his life with me is what I'd be worrying about,' says Nora. 'After all, I'd be the one that was to blame.'

'Never mind about him at all, now, girl,' Joan says with a jolly laugh. 'It's my own troubles that I'm thinking about.

Honestly, do you know, I don't think I could face it!'

'I'm full sure I couldn't,' says Nora, lighting a cigarette.

'But what else could you do?' Marie asks. She obviously thinks they are two very peculiar girls, and no wonder. They were peculiar, like all delightful girls.

'Do you know, Marie,' says Joan, 'I think I'd sooner marry the first poor devil that came the way.'

'Aren't you lucky, being able to pick them up like that?' Marie asks dryly.

'Ah, well, Marie,' says Joan, 'a girl would be in a bad way entirely if there wasn't one man that would take her on.'

'Like Paddy Lacy,' says Nora, with a giggle. 'He stopped me on the road the other day while he was delivering the letters, and I declare to God I didn't know which way to look.'

'I see,' says Marie. 'So that's why you keep Paddy Lacy on. I was wondering about that.'

'You needn't,' Nora says with sudden temper. 'I'm pretty sure Paddy Lacy would be just as tough as the rest of them if I went along and told him a thing like that.'

'But why would you have to tell him, Nora?' Joan asks anxiously. 'Wouldn't you let him find out for himself?'

'And a nice situation I'd be in when he did!'

'Oh, I wouldn't be too sure,' Joan says with another laugh. 'Before a man made up his mind about a thing like that, I'd like him to have a chance of seeing the full beauty of my character. Like the boatman in Glengarriff, I'm at my best on a long stretch.'

'I think I'd as soon live with a man I forced to marry me as one I tricked into marrying me,' Nora says. 'And I'd sooner do either than what your pal did – farm out a child. I don't think I'd ever have a day's luck after.'

'Now, you're misjudging the girl there, Nora,' Joan says earnestly. 'You are, really! It's not the same thing when you never have the chance of getting attached to a child. And when there isn't a blessed thing you can do about it, I don't honestly believe that there's any moral responsibility.'

'Responsibility?' Nora says, getting up. 'Who's talking about responsibility? I'd live in dread of my own shadow for the rest of my days. I wouldn't be able to see a barefooted kid in the street without getting sick. Every knock that came to the door, I'd be in dread to open it. Every body that was picked out of the river, I'd feel it was my kid, and I was the one to blame. For God's sake, don't talk to me!'

'There's another cup of tea left, Nora,' Joan says, a little too brightly. 'Would you like it?'

'In a minute, Joan,' says Nora, and goes out to the Ladies'. When she returns a few minutes later, she looks as though she had been crying. To me it is a great mystery, because no one speaks crossly to her. I assume that, like myself, she has a father who drinks.

'Cripes, I'm sorry for poor May Jenkins,' Joan begins on another day, after Nora has poured out the tea. That is her time for a new theme, when there is no serious danger of interruption.

'Who's *she* when she's at home?' Nora asks lightly.

'May Jenkins? You'd hardly know her, Norah. She's from the south side.'

'And what ails her now didn't ail her before?' asks Nora, who is full of local quips and phrases.

'Oh, the usual thing,' says Joan with a shrug. 'Phil Macken, her husband, is knocking round with the Archer girl, on the Wellington Road – the Yellow Peril.'

'Really, Joan,' Marie says, 'I don't know where you come across all those extraordinary people.'

'I don't see what's so extraordinary about that at all,' Nora says. 'People are always doing it.'

'And people are always getting terrible diseases, only we don't go out of our way to inquire,' says Marie primly. 'Really, there must be something wrong with a woman like that.'

'Like May, Marie?' Joan asks in mock surprise.

'No, like that other creature – whatever you said her name was.'

'Oh, I wouldn't say that at all, Marie,' says Joan. 'Some very respectable people live on the Wellington Road. And a lot of men find her attractive.'

'Then there must be something wrong with the men.'

'Or the wife, why don't you say?' cries Nora.

'Or the wife,' Marie agrees, with perfect placidity. 'She should be able to mind her own husband.'

'She'd want roller skates,' says Joan, and again I hear the high note of the violin, driving the trio onward. 'No, Marie, girl,' she says, resting her chin on her hands, 'you have to face the facts. A lot of women do get unattractive after marriage. Of course, I'm not blaming them. We'd be the same ourselves, with kids to mind and jobs to do. They can't waste time dancing and dolling themselves up like Maeve Archer, and if they did, their houses would soon show it. You see, it's something we all have to be prepared for.'

'If I felt that way, Joan, I'd go into a convent,' Marie says severely.

'But after all, Marie,' says Joan, 'what could you do? Suppose you were married to Jim and a thing like that happened?'

'What could I do?' Marie echoes, smiling at the thought of anything of the sort happening with Jim. 'Well, I suppose I could walk out of the house.'

'Ah, come now, Marie,' Joan says. 'It's not as easy as all that. Where would you walk to, in the first place?'

'What's wrong with going home?'

'With a houseful of kids?' says Joan. 'Of course, I know your father is very fond of you and all the rest of it, but all the same, we have to be reasonable.'

'I could go somewhere else,' says Marie. 'After all, Jim would have to support me – and the kids, as you say.'

'Of course he would. That's if you didn't mind spending the rest of your days as a grass widow. You know, Marie, I saw one or two women who did that, and it didn't look too promising to me. No, in the way of husbands and fathers

and so on, I don't think you can beat men. A dog won't
do.'

'But do you mean you'd let him go on seeing a filthy creature like that?' asks Marie. 'Really, Joan, I don't think you can
be serious.'

'Oh, I never said that,' Joan says hastily, 'I'm sure I'd make
it pretty uncomfortable for him.'

'Which mightn't be such a bad way of making the other
woman more attractive,' Nora says dryly.

'Oh, we all know what Nora would do,' Joan retorts with
affectionate mockery. 'She'd sit down and have a good cry.
Wouldn't you, love?'

'I might,' Nora replies doubtfully. 'I'd sooner that than
calling in the neighbours.'

'Oh, I admit you'd have to keep your dignity, Nora,' Marie
says, being particularly susceptible to any appeal to her lady-
hood. 'But surely someone would have to interfere.'

'I saw too much interference, Marie,' Nora says grimly.
'It's mad enough thinking you can spend your whole life
with a man and still be in love with him, but 'tis dotty
entirely if you imagine you can do it with half Cork acting
as referee.'

'All the same, Nora,' Joan says, in her practical way,
'before I saw a woman like that making off with a husband
of mine, I'd get a fistful of her hair, and I wouldn't mind
who knew it, either. I'd read and spell her, I give you my
word.'

'I certainly wouldn't degrade myself by quarrelling with
a creature like that,' says Marie.

'I wouldn't have the nerve,' says Nora, lighting a cigarette.
'Look, it's all very well to talk about it like that, but suppose
it was the other way around? Suppose you were making a
fool of yourself over another man, and your husband disgraced you all over Cork by fighting him?'

'Really, Nora,' says Marie, with her Mona Lisa smile, 'you
have a remarkably vivid imagination.'

'Oh, I don't know that that's all imagination, either,

Marie,' says Joan, who enjoys nothing better than imagining things. 'That could happen, too, mind you!'

'But that would make you no better than the woman you're just talking about,' says Marie.

'Who said we were any better?' asks Nora. 'I might be worse, for all anyone knows.'

'But do you know, Nora,' Joan says, 'I'm not at all sure but I'd like Mick to do it.'

'To shame you all over Cork?' Nora asks.

'Oh, no. Just to stand up for his rights. Nobody wants a doormat.'

'Give me doormats every time,' says Nora, with a sinister pull at her cigarette.

'But, Nora,' Marie asks in horror, 'you don't mean you'd just sit at home and do nothing?'

'I don't know, girl. What could you do?'

'And wait till he changed his mind and came back to you?'

'Maybe,' says Nora, with a shrug. 'I mightn't be there when he got back. I might have a fellow, too.'

'Really,' Marie says, scratching her long neck. 'I'm beginning to see a number of uses for this Paddy Lacy of yours.'

'That's where women have the worst of it,' Joan says quickly, to head off a reply from Nora about Paddy Lacy. 'It's not as easy for a married woman with a couple of kids to find someone to go off with. It's too chancy giving children a stepfather, no matter how fond you might be of him. No, what I can't imagine,' she adds earnestly, 'is what you'd do when he did change his mind. I often wonder could you ever behave in the same way to him.'

'Of course not, Joan,' Marie says. 'Naturally, if there were children, I could understand remaining in the same house with him, just for their sake, but living with him as husband and wife is a thing I could never imagine doing.'

'Ah, now, Marie, you're a girl of great character,' Joan says, 'but that sounds to me too much like giving up sweets in a sweetshop. Of course, I know people do it when they get tired of one another, but it never seems natural to me. I wouldn't do it just for fun,' she adds gravely. 'I'd want to be pretty sure that he was still fond of me.'

'I'm afraid I wouldn't have much faith in the affections of a man like that,' Marie says.

'What about you, Nora?' Joan asks.

'Me?' Nora says, blushing. 'Oh, I suppose 'twould depend.'

'You mean, depend on how he behaved to you?'

'Yes,' Nora replies with a frightened air. 'And how he behaved to the other one.'

'Well, really, Nora, this is going beyond the beyonds!' Marie exclaims, putting down her cup with a ladylike air of finality. 'Are we supposed to take *her* feelings into consideration as well?'

'I suppose she might have feelings, too?' Nora replies gloomily.

'I know what Nora would do!' Joan says triumphantly, bringing her hand down flat on the table. 'I know it just as if I was there. She'd tell her husband to go to blazes, and skelp off to the other woman's house to console her.'

'By the way she's talking, it sounds as if she'd leave her husband and live with the other one,' Marie says.

'I might even do that,' says Nora, moving towards the door.

'Ah, go on, girl!' Joan says boisterously. 'Don't you know we're only making fun of you? I know what's going to happen to you,' she adds comfortingly. 'You'll marry a fine steady slob of a man that'll stick his two heels on the mantelpiece and never look at the side of the road another woman is walking at. Look, there's a cup of tea in the pot still!'

'I don't want it, Joanie, thanks,' says Nora, and goes off to the Ladies'.

Marie gives a shrug. 'For an intelligent girl, Nora does talk the most extraordinary nonsense,' she says with finality.

'Oh, I wouldn't be too sure it was nonsense, Marie,' Joan says, in her loyal way. 'I think Nora might surprise us all.'

But Nora, worse luck, has never had the opportunity of surprising anyone; nor has Joan – two fine women who have never met with men astute enough to grab them. As for Marie, she rules her husband gently but firmly, like a reverend mother dealing with a rather dull undergardener. Of the three, she is now the one I am most intimate with. Sometimes I even think that if I were to forget myself and make advances to her, instead of slapping my face indignantly she would only laugh and say, 'Ah, Larry, will you have a bit of sense?' – which from Marie would be almost like a declaration of love. And I think the reason is that like me, she hears those voices 'vibrate in the memory' and wonders over them.

'Ah, Larry,' she says, grabbing me eagerly by the hands, 'do you remember all the old nonsense we used to talk in the office, and Joan saying what she'd do with an illegitimate baby, and me saying what I'd do if Jim went off with another woman? And look at us now – three old women!'

No doubt she realized that she can afford to say things like that to me, for while the music of those voices lingers in my mind she and they will never be old.

(1958)

SUE

GOD forgive me, I could never stand my sister's young men. Even if she had had taste, I should still have resented them. Our house on the outskirts of Cork was small, and there simply wasn't room in it for me and a courting couple. After a day's work in the office I would get settled with a book by the fire in the front room, and then I would hear the creak of the gate, the steps on the path, the knock, the boisterous voice in the hall – my hall! Sometimes I continued to read, and dared the fellow to come in and interrupt me, but there was never any false modesty about Sue's young men. They always had a warm corner in their hearts for themselves. Occasionally I went off to read in the kitchen, but there, apart from Mother's solicitude about whether I was warm enough and whether I could see with 'the old gas' – meaning the gaslight fixture that I was reading by – I was almost certain to be interrupted again by the arrival of one of her old cronies, come to sit and gossip with her in the kitchen. So, most often, when I heard Sue's young man, I went off, cursing, to my own bedroom, where there was no heat and 'the old gas' was worse even than in the kitchen. There, lying on my bed with a blanket over my feet, I listened to the cheerful voices of Sue and her young man sitting in comfort downstairs before the fire – my fire! Is it any wonder I grew lepping mad? Sue, of course, said I was sulky and unsociable, and Mother, who had an excuse for everybody, said the Horgans were all like that. I grew up with a considerable respect for the sensitiveness and intelligence of the Horgans.

Sue never had any taste in young men. There was a long string of them, only one of whom I ever liked, and she dropped him inside a fortnight. She said he was dull! Mind, I had no very exaggerated notion of *her* charms. I knew she wasn't steady and was always excited or depressed about something, and when she had nothing to be excited or depressed about, she came up with the most extraordinary old pisherogues and superstitions that were supposed to be lucky or unlucky, according to the mood she was in. But she was warmhearted and generous, and she had a very good intelligence whenever the fancy took her to be intelligent. At any rate she was a cut above the fellows she walked out with, though it wasn't until Harry Ridgeway came on the scene that I began to appreciate what an interesting girl she was.

I had also better be fair and admit that Ridgeway had his points, even though I didn't like him. I always thought him a bit too much of a dandy. He had a pink-and-white complexion like a girl's, and he dressed as carefully as any girl. Usually he wore a well-cut, tight-fitting suit that never had a trace of beer or tobacco ash on it, and a pale, correct-looking tie. And he had the impudence to jeer at my tweeds and my battered old tie and about how I needed a haircut. At a party he was always in charge of entertaining the dolls, while I sat with a couple of friends and a half-dozen of stout hidden behind the sofa, and hoped to God the dolls would let us alone to talk politics or religion. Ridgeway had no politics, and his religion was like his ties – pale and correct. What I really mean is that he was a lightweight, a ladies' man, though with occasional flashes of wit and intelligence, but definitely not the sort with whom you'd like to go to a bar and spend the evening discussing what was wrong with the country.

Still, I was rather puzzled by Sue's behaviour, because, though she went out quite a lot with Ridgeway, she continued to go out as well with Sidney Healy, who had now been the resident pest for close on six months. I saw no reason for having two of them about the house, disturbing me.

'Are you going steady with that masher?' I asked her one evening while she was ironing and Mother washing up.

'What masher?' she asked, growing nervous and defensive, though I hadn't even raised my voice.

'How do you expect me to remember all their names? The sickly fellow with the queer ties.'

'Harry Ridgeway?' she said in the same tone. 'Why would I go steady with him? Sure, he's mad on Judy Holmes.'

'Then why the hell doesn't he go to Judy Holmes' house instead of coming here?' I asked. 'Who is this Holmes one, anyway?'

'She's the bank manager's daughter from Montenotte.'

'Old Holmes' daughter?' I asked in surprise. 'But aren't they Protestants?'

'I suppose they are. What about it?'

'Nothing, only he's not going to find it very easy to marry her, is he?'

'I don't know. I suppose he can get a dispensation. They have money enough, anyway. I advised him to propose to her months ago.'

'Very handsome of you, I'm sure,' I said with a sniff.

'There's nothing handsome about it. She's the right sort of girl for him, and she has a bit of money. The poor devil is crazy to get out of that house of his. His old fellow drinks, and his poor mother is in and out of hospital the whole time.'

'I see,' I said. 'And because Mr Ridgeway isn't happy at home, he thinks he's entitled to come and make sure that I'm not happy here.'

That evening I didn't move when Ridgeway came in. It's bad enough getting out of a comfortable room for another man, but at least you have the feeling that one of these days things are going to even out. But to let him have it as a free gift – chair, fire, gaslight, and all – was more than anyone could expect. Ridgeway didn't seem to resent my staying, and except for that silly-looking tie of his and his mincing way of balancing a teacup on his knee, I had nothing to complain of. The man had plenty of conversation, of a kind. Later in the evening Sue asked him about Judy Holmes, and he didn't seem to resent that, either.

'Oh, Judy's playing at the School of Music concert next week,' he said excitedly.

'Go on!' said Sue. 'What's she playing?'

'The Mozart E-flat, with Humphreys doing the violin part.'

'Cripes, I'd love to hear her,' said Sue.

'We can go together, if you like. What about you, Jack?'

'No, thanks,' I said with a smile. I was fond of music, all right, but I avoided the local amateurs.

However, when Sue returned from the concert, she was full of Judy Holmes, and I knew there must have been something to her playing, for Sue in one of her intelligent phases was quite a good critic. She could have been a good pianist as well, but, being Sue, she never took the trouble to practise. She sat at the piano to illustrate what she was saying, and I filled in the violin part with three fingers while she showed how Judy did it, and when she played a wrong chord she used a dirty word. I laughed. I was always amused at the contrast between Sue's character and the language she used.

In a funny way, hearing about the concert gave me a sort of personal interest in the Holmes girl, and next time I met her in town I raised my cap to her. She smiled back rather coolly, and I wondered if she even knew who I was. She was a tall, thin girl with a long, pale face, and a good figure concealed in a wide coat like a tent. Her hat was a plain felt one, like a schoolgirl's. She was dressed expensively, but plainly. After that, whenever I found myself daydreaming, I would think of her as the sort of girl you could take up as you took up politics or religion – a girl of natural seriousness, who could play Mozart as he should be played, and

with no nonsense about her. Now when Ridgeway talked
about her to Mother and Sue, I found myself listening to
him. They were fascinated by everything he told them about
the Holmeses, and it wasn't only the money and the bit of
style that interested them, though clearly, for them as for
Ridgeway, it had the appeal of a fairytale. But besides this
they both had a genuine admiration for the qualities of
character the Holmeses displayed: Judy's daily two hours of
piano practice, her dutifulness in answering letters and remembering birthdays, her mother's social work, and the
strict and narrow piety of an Irish Protestant family. How
narrow that could be I was reminded one night when
Ridgeway reported that one of Judy's girlfriends had used a
Biblical phrase by way of a joke and Mrs Holmes had
pointed out that it was blasphemy.

'Sure, when the girl didn't mean it!' protested Mother,
who never really minded what people said so long as they
smiled at her while they were saying it.

'Ah, they don't look at it that way at all, Mrs Horgan,'
Ridgeway said with a frown. 'Of course the girl didn't mean
it, but still they don't think you should say such things. And
I can't help admiring them for it.'

I could see that Ridgeway had Mother and Sue admiring
them for it as well.

But then an extraordinary thing happened. Ridgeway
proposed, but he proposed not to Judy, but to Sue. I couldn't
understand it. I knew that he wanted to make a home of his
own, and it wasn't only that his father drank and his mother
was so sickly that she could not keep abreast of the housekeeping. He wanted a background to go with the ties and
suits, and he must have been miserably selfconscious about
any friends that called to his house. You could see the sort of
place he would try and make for himself—a small house in a
modern terrace, with a neatly covered suite of furniture,
bought on time, a few watercolours, and a vase of flowers;
and there he would give little musical parties, and tea would
be served in rather dainty cups. But Sue's background was

just the same as his own, and imagine Sue keeping a house like that for him. She would wreck the damn place in a week.

I could see that the proposal had come as a real shock to Sue. She couldn't understand it, either, and as a result she couldn't stop talking of it.

'But you like him,' I said. 'Why shouldn't you marry him if you want to?'

'Ah, how could I?' she asked doubtfully. 'He's not in love with me. Isn't that enough?'

'How sure you are of it!' I said. I wasn't really any fonder of Ridgeway than I had been, but I realized that he would make someone an excellent husband and that Sue was the sort of girl who might very easily marry the wrong man – or no man at all. 'Isn't that for him to say?'

'Ah, it's not that,' she said, and she still sounded doubtful. 'I suppose he felt he had to ask me.'

'He needn't have felt that at all,' Mother said earnestly, 'but it showed very nice feeling. I was always very fond of Harry, and I only wish you could marry him.'

'Oh, for God's sake, hold on!' I said, getting angry with them again. 'I don't think Sue even knows what she's doing. Nobody ever proposes to a girl just out of nice feeling.'

'Harry would,' Sue said flatly. 'He's too soft for his own good. I dare say he thought people were talking about us.'

'Nonsense!' I said shortly. 'He knows more about girls than that. Probably he proposed to Judy Holmes and got the cold shoulder.'

'I wouldn't say so,' Sue said thoughtfully. 'I think he'd have told me.'

'For a man you won't marry you seem to have a remarkably high opinion of him,' I said sarcastically. 'I'd wait and see about that.'

'Ah, I don't think so,' Sue said complacently. 'Even if he did propose to her, she'd hardly talk about it.'

'She'd be the first woman in history that didn't,' said I.

'I wouldn't be too sure about that, either,' said Sue. 'Harry probably has his own reasons for not proposing to her. I dare say his family wouldn't like his marrying a Protestant.'

And suddenly she rang a bell in my head. You see, there were certain things that I seemed always to have known about myself. One was that if I fell in love there would be no walking out with other girls. Another was that if I did fall in love with someone I knew my family and friends would disapprove of – a Jew or a Protestant – I would not allow myself to be influenced by them. Whatever other faults I might have, I knew myself to be a man of seriousness and strength of character. And these, I knew, were precisely the qualities that Ridgeway hadn't got.

'Ah, so that's the reason! I said, and I dare say triumph showed in my voice, for Sue turned on me.

'And what's wrong with it?' she asked.

'Nothing,' I said. 'Except that now you're talking sense.'

I liked that explanation because it enabled me to go on looking down on Ridgeway. But I still couldn't understand why Sue didn't want to marry him when, quite clearly, she liked him so much. I knew that she wasn't acting like the heroine of a sentimental novel and refusing him for fear of injuring his career. Apart from anything else, Sue had never read enough novels to know that a heroine might be expected to act in this peculiar way, and if you had explained it to her, she would merely have gaped and asked in her commonest tone, 'What sort of bloody idiot do you think I am?' No, the girl had got it firmly fixed in her head that Ridgeway didn't care for her, and for that reason would not marry him.

Yet they continued to go out together. After his proposal, I felt that Ridgeway was entitled to whatever facilities the house offered, and I left the parlour to them. One night, I was sitting with Mother in the kitchen. Sue and Ridgeway were supposed to be courting in the front room. All at once a most unholy row began. We couldn't hear what they said, but he was talking in a low, bitter voice and Sue was yelling her head off at him. Mother clasped her hands in prayer and made to get up, but I signalled to her to stay where she was.

'The poor child!' Mother moaned. 'God direct me!' she added, meaning that she distrusted my direction. The sitting-room door opened and I distinctly heard Ridgeway use a dirty word. Two dirty words! Fortunately, Mother either didn't hear or didn't understand. Then the front door slammed behind him, and Mother, with another glance at the ceiling, from which God could be supposed to be directing her, muttered, 'And without even saying goodnight to me!' It was a real tragedy for Mother, because she loved Harry Ridgeway's little airs of politeness, so different from the roughness of Sue and me. Then Sue came into the kitchen, bawling, and for five minutes it was impossible to get a stime of sense out of her.

'Child!' Mother cried, with what she clearly believed to be sternness. 'You must tell your brother and me what he said to you.' When she referred to me as Sue's brother, she promoted me to a position of authority.

'He asked me to marry him again,' sobbed Sue.

Mother, being one of the sympathetic souls of the world, was just on the point of saying 'The blackguard! He should be ashamed of himself!' when she realized that it wouldn't be altogether appropriate, so she just wrung her hands and said, 'Well! Well! Well!'

'After all, that's nothing to snivel about,' I said coldly.

'Who's snivelling?' Sue asked, flaring up, as I had expected her to do. 'He said things were desperate in his house. It's not the only bloody house things are desperate in, if you ask me.'

'Oh, Sue—' Mother was beginning when I broke in.

'And what did you tell him?'

'The same thing I told him before, of course. So he said he was going straight off to ask Judy Holmes.'

'All right,' I said. 'And isn't that what you wanted?'

'Whether I wanted it or not has nothing to do with it,' she

said. 'How the hell could I marry a fellow like that, that would hate the very sight of me before the honeymoon was over?'

'Oh, Sue, how can you say things like that?' Mother exclaimed indignantly.

'Because it's true, woman. I know Jack thinks he is a bit of a snob. What's wrong with that? Ye're all terrified out of your lives of trying to make yourself out a bit better than ye are. I'd be a snob, too, if only I had something to be a snob about. He hates a girl even to use a dirty word.'

'And perfectly right he is!' Mother cried. 'What right has any decent girl to use language like that, picked up at street corners?'

'Then what does he want with me? He heard me use it. He told me if I ever used a word like that again he'd slap my face.'

'And what did you do?' I asked, knowing perfectly well what Sue would do if I told her that.

'I said it, of course.'

'Sue, you didn't!' exclaimed Mother.

'I did,' said Sue, and then began to giggle faintly.

'And what did he do?' I asked.

'Oh, he slapped my face, all right,' said Sue, her face lighting up. Obviously the incident had made a favourable impression. 'What should he do?'

'He should talk to you seriously, Sue,' Mother said passionately. 'He should not do a thing like that. I'm surprised at him – such a nice boy! Eleven years I lived with your poor father, God rest him, and never once did he lift a hand to me.'

'A pity he didn't lift it to us a bit oftener,' said Sue.

'The dear knows, it's hard to know what to do,' Mother said, turning away and shaking her head despondently.

'Anyway,' I said, realizing what was in Sue's mind, 'you know he's not going to ask Judy.'

'That's all you know about him,' Sue replied, beginning to sob again. 'He's probably asking her now. And she's the right girl for him, whatever his family or anyone else thinks.'

Then she went up to her room to live it all through again, and bawl a bit more, while Mother sat by the fire and sighed over the contrariness of everything. Of course, she knew that Sue was doing the right thing, but she couldn't help wishing she wasn't. As for me, I was beginning to make discoveries about my extraordinary sister. I knew now that she had refused to marry Harry Ridgeway because she genuinely believed he didn't care for her. The poor fool had so often expressed his admiration for Judy and her family that he had even persuaded those two romantic women to admire them as well, and Sue could only think of love in terms of admiration. Admiration, that is, of positive virtues she recognized and respected. She was quite certain that she had none of those particular virtues herself, and yet she would keep on hoping that some day some man would discover something positive to admire in her. Perhaps, after all, she wasn't even so extraordinary; perhaps a lot of other women confuse love and admiration in the same way, and never realize that a man may love them as much for their faults as their virtues, and may think with delight of the way they begin to sparkle when everyone else is going home, or forget themselves and swear. At the same time, I knew it was something I should never be able to explain to Sue, and for some reason this made me feel unusually tender to her in the weeks that followed. I even took her to the pictures a couple of times, when she and everyone else knew I hated the pictures.

But she had been right about Harry Ridgeway. That night or next day he had gone straight to Judy Holmes and proposed to her and been accepted. He'd even induced herself and her family to sign along the dotted line in connexion with the religion of the children. I had to admit that when it came to the point, Ridgeway, ties and all, was masculine enough.

It might have been better for him if he hadn't been. I met the pair of them one night on Patrick's Bridge. She was, as usual, plainly dressed, while Ridgeway was even more the dandy than before. Between them they made me feel very awkward, with my long hair, my cap, and my rough tweeds, but Ridgeway seemed very pleased to meet me.

'You've heard of Sue's brother, Jack,' he said to Judy.

'Almost as much as I've heard of Sue,' she said with a thin smile. 'I suppose he's another charmer?'

'Oh, begod, he is not,' Ridgeway said with a loud laugh. 'Sourest blackguard you'll find about this town.'

'Ah, he probably only needs a girl to make a lot of him, as you do of Sue,' she said archly.

'Come on, Holmes!' he cried. 'You never heard the half of Sue.'

'No, you didn't get much chance of telling about her, did you, poor fellow?' she said in a mocking drawl. 'But you do get these dreadful obsessions with people.'

We said goodnight, and I went on through town. It was only when I was halfway down Patrick Street that it dawned on me that Judy hadn't been exactly pleasant to me. For some reason I always approached people on the assumption that they intend to be nice to me, and it usually takes time before I realize that they haven't been. I had gone the full length of the street before I thought, 'My God, that girl is a devil!'

As I strolled home that night, I could see as clearly as if I were living through it how dearly Ridgeway was going to pay for his harmless snobbery. I could also see why he might have been afraid of bringing a girl like that into his own family. People of our class are plain and rough, but nobody is so plain and rough that they wouldn't resent her tone, and from this time on Ridgeway would have to depend for his friendships on his wife's family and their friends.

I was so full of my own discovery that while I was telling Mother and Sue, it never once struck me that they might feel differently about it. They listened in silence, and then Sue lit a cigarette and said, 'God damn her!' and Mother didn't even protest. She was too shaken. 'The poor, deluded boy!' she said softly, clasping and unclasping her hands.

Then I saw that both had tears in their eyes, not only for Harry Ridgeway and his aspirations but for their own. It was as if life had betrayed them by being less generous than they themselves were. I kissed them before I went to bed. It was not a custom of mine, but I felt extraordinarily proud of them both.

(1958)

A MOTHER'S WARNING

ONE winter evening Father Fogarty's housekeeper let in a strange young woman. She was tall and thin with a slight pale face, and her good manners barely contained a natural excitability of manner. Though he was normally shy of women he was attracted by her and offered her coffee.

'When you know what I came about you probably won't ask me to have coffee,' she replied with a rueful grin.

'In that case I'd better order it first,' he said, responding to her tone.

'You'd better hear what I have to confess and *then* order it,' she suggested slyly.

'By the way, it's not Confession you want, is it?' he asked professionally.

'That comes afterwards too, like the coffee,' she replied.

'I don't know what your name is yet,' he said as she sat down.

'Sheila Moriarty.'

'You're not from this part of the world?'

'No. I'm from Limerick. I'm working here in Carr's Stores.'

'How do you like it?'

'The shop is all right. The place itself is fine. Too fine. I suppose that's what got me into the mess I'm in. Oh, I didn't realize it in time, but I was probably brought up too sheltered.'

'How many of you are there?' he asked.

'Six. Three boys, three girls. Daddy is an insurance agent; Mummy – well, I suppose Mummy is a saint.'

'A what?' he asked in surprise.

'Oh, I don't mean it that way, but she is, really. Trying to bring up six of us on Daddy's couple of quid and see that we had everything – education, music, religion. I'm damn full sure I couldn't do it. Now, here I am after less than a year away bringing disgrace on her!'

'What did you do?' he asked quietly.

'Stole stuff from the shop,' she replied sullenly. In Fogarty's experience there were two sorts of women criers, the ones who cried at once and the ones who got sullen. She was the sort who got sullen. 'Nice, aren't I?' she asked with a bitter little smile.

For a few moments he could say nothing. With her looks and temperament he would have expected her to say that she was pregnant, but you could never tell with women.

'How serious is it?' he asked gravely, and she opened her handbag and put a brooch on the little table beside her. It looked to him as silly as any other brooch – a sort of golden leaf that he couldn't imagine anyone's risking a job for.

'How much is it worth?' he asked doubtfully.

'Three quid,' she said.

'Can't you put it back?' he asked, and she shook her head slowly.

'I'm in a different department now.'

'Or put the price of it in the till?'

'Not without its being spotted.'

'All right,' he said. 'Send them a postal order anonymously. They won't ask any questions.'

'It's not as simple as that,' she said. 'Somebody knows I stole it.'

'Oh!' he exclaimed. 'Somebody in the shop?'

'Yes. An assistant manager. He encouraged me, in fact. He said the whole staff did it. Maybe they do; I don't know, but it doesn't matter anyhow. I should have known better.'

'I take it this manager fellow is a man?'

'Yes. His name is Michael Joyce. He lives in St Mary's Road.'

'Is he married by any chance?'

That did it. She began to sob dryly and bitterly. Then she dabbed her nose viciously with a handkerchief and went on talking as though at random.

'Cripes, and before I left home Mummy told me never to take anything that belonged to my employers. I went into hysterics on her. It shows you the way we were brought up. I didn't know people could do things like that. And *then* she told me not to have anything to do with married men because they weren't all like Daddy! We always thought she was so blooming innocent. She wasn't as innocent as we were, though.'

'You'd better tell me the rest of this,' Fogarty said sternly. 'How far has this thing gone?'

'Too far.'

'You mean you and he have been living together?'

'Near enough to it anyway. And that's what he wants.'

'But it's not what you want?'

'Not now,' she said almost angrily. 'At first, I suppose I let myself be dazzled. I must have when I let him persuade me to pinch that, mustn't I? Now that I know what he's like I'd sooner pitch myself in the river.'

'What is he like?' Fogarty asked.

'Oh, he's not what you think,' she said ruefully. 'He's clever. I know he's smooth and he's a liar, but he could probably get round you too if it was worth his while.'

'What do you mean when you say he's a liar?' Fogarty asked, weighing it up.

'I mean he told me things about his wife, and *they* were lies.'

'How do you know?'

'Because I met her.'

'Oh, so you know his wife?'

'I do. He made me come to his house one night after work for a bit of supper. It nearly choked me. That was when I turned against him. He brought me there deliberately to show me off to her. He watched us the whole time. And everything he'd said was wrong. She was decent and she was as frightened of him as I was. There's a devil in that man.'

'Is that all?' he asked.

'Isn't it enough?' she retorted. 'I think only for that last evening he could have done what he liked with me. But he isn't normal.'

'I mean, could we have the coffee in now?' he asked with an encouraging smile. Then he went to the head of the stairs and bellowed, 'Mary! Coffee!' He shut the room door behind him and swaggered back to the mantelpiece. 'I'll have to think what's the best thing to do,' he said, sounding more confident than he felt. 'About this, to begin with,' he added, picking up the brooch. 'I gather you have no further use for it?'

'I wish to God I'd never seen it,' she said.

'You won't see it again,' he said, and put it in his coat pocket. 'I have to think about Mr Joyce as well. Meanwhile, whatever you do, don't go anywhere with him. Don't even talk to him. If he annoys you, tell him to go to hell. I suppose he's trying to blackmail you over the brooch?'

'I suppose so, in a way,' she replied uncertainly. 'He's not as crude as that, of course.'

'They never are,' he said from the depths of his worldly wisdom. 'But remember, there's nothing he can do to you that wouldn't injure himself a great deal worse.'

'I wouldn't be too sure of that,' she said doubtfully. 'A fellow in a position like that doesn't have to say, "Miss Moriarty stole a brooch from the jewellery counter." '

'I don't think he'll say anything,' Fogarty said forcefully. 'Does he know you were coming to me?'

'No. I never told him anything.'

'If he starts anything, tell him I know everything about it,' he said. 'There's nothing these fellows dread more than a third party who's in on the game. Meanwhile forget about it. But remember, next time you meet a married man, what your mother told you. They're *not* all like your father. She was right there.'

When they had drunk their coffee he saw her to the door and held her hand for a moment.

'Give me two days to see what I can do,' he said. 'I'll be here on Friday night if you want me. Until then, forget about it.'

But this was more than he could do himself. Fogarty, partly because of his character, partly because of his circumstance, was a man who lived a great deal in his own imagination, and something about the girl had set his imagination on fire. Even the few words she had dropped had made him see the sort of home she came from, and the anxious, pious mother who tried to spread out her husband's little income into a full and comfortable life for six children who probably didn't even realize the sacrifices she was making for them, and wouldn't realize it till she was dead and buried. 'A saint,' the girl had said, and she was probably right. He had known saints like that whose lives nobody would ever know about, much less write about. He could even see how a girl brought up in a poor, pious, cheerful home like that, where no quarrel was ever allowed to occur that could not be reported later as a joke to friends, and who was then left alone in a cheerless town would be readier than the next to grasp at whatever society offered itself. And he had no difficulty at all in imagining the sinister figure of Joyce, trying to lure the girl from one small misdemeanour to another until eventually he could exercise a moral blackmail on her. He had seen a few men like that as well. What would have happened to the girl if she hadn't had the sense to consult a priest required no imagination at all. But, in spite of his burning determination to frustrate Joyce, he wasn't at all sure what he should do.

Clearly, the first thing was to get some information, and the following evening he called on the curate in Joyce's parish. He was a tall, gentle young man called Rowlands, with whom Fogarty had spent a few months in another part of the diocese.

'Information, Ed!' Fogarty said. 'Information about one of your parishioners!'

'I'm sorry, Jerry, but the seal of the confessional is strictly observed in this parish,' Rowlands said with his old-maidish humour. 'Who is it, tell me?'

'A fellow called Joyce in St Mary's Road.'

'A manager in Carr's?' Rowlands said, stroking his long jaw thoughtfully. 'I know the man you mean. He's a small, bouncy little chap. It wouldn't be woman trouble, would it?'

'Why?' Fogarty asked keenly. 'Did he have woman trouble?'

'Oh, I heard something I didn't pay much attention to. About two years ago. He used to be a traveller for Carr's before he got the big job.'

'Anything else?'

'Let me see! It's coming back to me. Mind you, I couldn't say it was anything but old talk. He was supposed to be having something to do with a married woman called Trench. She was a Protestant, of course. Anyway, herself and her husband left in a hurry. Is that the sort of thing?'

'More or less,' Fogarty said grimly. 'This time it isn't a Protestant, and I see no reason why the woman should leave town in a hurry. Don't you think I'm right?'

'Oh, I'm sure you are, but all the same I'd be careful, Jerry. That sort of thing can get you into a nasty mess.'

'Ah, aren't I always careful?' Fogarty said with a jolly laugh.

'You are,' Rowlands said cautiously, 'but in unorthodox ways. I'm very orthodox, Jerry. I like to go by the books.'

But Fogarty had heard what he came to hear and his mind was made up. Next morning he rang Joyce up at the shop and suggested that it might be more convenient for both if they met that evening at the presbytery. Joyce fell in with this enthusiastically and arrived that evening at the presbytery, looking as though he hoped to sell Fogarty a new suite of furniture. As a subtle touch Fogarty had left the stolen brooch lying on the little table where Sheila had placed it, but he was disappointed in his hope of seeing Joyce discountenanced. He smiled and picked up the brooch.

'That's a nice little article, Father,' he said. 'Fifty bob in the store.'

'Three pounds, I believe,' Fogarty said sternly.

'As much as that?' Joyce said, in what appeared to be genuine surprise. 'Probably costs four and tuppence to make. But that's how we come to be millionaires, Father.'

'It belongs to the store,' said Fogarty. 'It might help to make millionaires of you quicker if you took it back there.'

'Me, Father?' Joyce asked innocently. 'Of course, I'll take it back if you like, but it might be a bit difficult to explain, mightn't it?'

'Oh, I wouldn't say so,' said Fogarty, beginning to lose his temper. 'You could tell them it was stolen at your instigation.'

'At my instigation?' Joyce repeated quietly. He took a few steps forward and faced Fogarty from the hearth, his arms folded. 'That's a very serious charge, Father,' he went on after a moment. 'Are you sure you're in a position to prove it?'

Fogarty was taken aback. The scene wasn't going at all as he had planned it; he was in no position to prove anything, and because of it he began to bluster.

'Yes, and you know who the witness would be,' he said angrily. 'Sheila Moriarty.'

'Sheila Moriarty?' Joyce repeated phrases and names in the manner of one who thinks while he talks, to give himself time. 'And do you think seriously, Father, that the Bishop is going to accept the story of a girl you say is a thief and consider that it entitled you to go round making wild charges against me?'

'You tried to seduce that girl,' shouted Fogarty, trying to brazen it out.

'And what else, Father?' Joyce asked impudently.

'I believe there is also a lady called Trench, who may have something to say about it,' Fogarty said furiously.

'I see,' Joyce said, but he didn't, again he was only playing for time. Then he suddenly changed from defence to attack, but even then he was very much master of himself as Fogarty was not.

'Has it struck you, Father, that Sheila is very well able to look after herself?'

'It hasn't,' Fogarty said shortly.

'Yet when she wants to be protected against me – that's her story, anyway, according to you – she goes to you and not the parish priest! Doesn't that seem peculiar?'

It didn't, so far as Fogarty was concerned. Whatever happened to Irish priests in the course of their career, young people who got into trouble always took care to avoid them when they became parish priests. And Dempsey, Fogarty's parish priest, was somebody whom anybody, old or young, would avoid.

'That's her business,' he said, raising his hand.

'You're trying to make it mine, Father,' Joyce said reproachfully. 'By the way, have you told the parish priest?'

'That's none of your business either,' Fogarty said, losing his temper again.

'Oh, but I might have to see the parish priest if this persecution went any further, Father.'

'Persecution?' Fogarty growled furiously.

'Yes, Father, persecution,' Joyce said steadily. 'Hysterical young women with sex on the brain going to young priests, who accept everything they say without making proper inquiries! That is persecution, and I hope it doesn't go any further. In the meantime,' Joyce added contemptuously, 'you'd be wise to put that brooch in the dustbin and forget about the whole business.' Then his tone changed again and became insolently personal. 'Before I go, Father, did Sheila Moriarty ever tell you what her mother's advice was before she left home?'

'I'm not discussing her business with you,' said Fogarty.

'You should really ask her some time,' said Joyce, and then he turned on his heel and went jauntily down the stairs.

Fogarty was furious. He knew he had been out-manoeuvred all over the shop, and by somebody he thoroughly despised and believed to be an arrant coward. He had an aching regret that he hadn't hit the man when he had the opportunity. It was clearly a public duty on some-one's part to hit him. But he had been foxed, and the result was that though he had summoned Joyce merely to warn him off, it was himself who had been warned off. And Fogarty was not a man who was accustomed to being warned off.

And yet, when he woke next morning, he was full of cheerfulness and bounce. When he analysed the scene all over again, everything about it seemed all right. An unpleasant duty had been done, no matter how inadequately. In spite of his bluff Joyce was a coward and much too afraid to pursue Sheila further. Above all, he would say nothing about the brooch. Sheila's word against his might not count, but Sheila's word and that of her priest would satisfy any reasonable person that he was at the bottom of any offence she had committed. But though Fogarty knew he had won, he realized too that for the future he must be more careful in his dealings with businessmen and would have to get advice, if not from the parish priest, at least from some priest older than himself. It was all very well to know a few thousand sins theoretically, but to know a few of them practically gave the other fellow an immense advantage.

When Sheila Moriarty came that evening she saw at once from his manner that things had gone well. This time he told Mary to bring up the coffee at once and till it arrived he talked to Sheila about her native place. When he had poured out the coffee he smiled knowingly at her.

'I had a visitor last night,' he said.

'What did you think of him?' she asked ruefully.

'To tell you the truth, I didn't like him very much. Smooth, of course. A smart salesman. Not one you could do business with, though.'

'Do you think I don't know it?' she asked wearily. 'What did he say for himself?'

'Nothing much for himself, a lot for other people. I'll be quite honest with you, he was too smart for me altogether, not to mind you. But I'm sure of one thing. He'll give you no more trouble unless you make an opportunity for him.'

'I promise you I won't do that if I can avoid it.'

'You'll have to avoid it,' Fogarty said sternly. 'Anything you have to do with that man for the future is going to injure you. He's frightened and sore, and he'll hurt you in any way he can.'

'And the brooch?'

'Never mind about that. Tell it in Confession, of course, but say you've taken steps to return it. I'll find a way myself sooner or later.'

'I'm not going to thank you,' she said. 'Only for you I don't know what would have happened me.'

'I did nothing only what I'd be bound to do for anyone,' he said. 'And even that much I mightn't have been able to do except that I knew something about him.'

'What was it?'

'Nothing much. Just an unfortunate married woman who found it advisable to leave town as a result of her association with him. That was something he didn't want brought up.'

'I suppose I should have guessed it,' she said despondently. 'It's our vanity that we can never bring ourselves to believe there could have been anyone else, isn't it? What else did he say?'

Fogarty realized with surprise that, bitter as she was, and perhaps because she was bitter, she could go on all night talking about Joyce.

'Oh, he told me to ask you what the advice was that your mother gave you,' Fogarty replied with a jolly laugh.

'He told you that?' she asked sharply, and at once he knew he had said the wrong thing. What there was wrong about it he couldn't see, unless it was that she was still so sore that every word she had uttered in confidence to a man she was in love with hurt her when it came from someone else.

'Naturally, I didn't say you'd already told me,' he added to comfort her.

'I'm glad of that anyway,' she said and got up.

'There's no need to go so soon,' he exclaimed. 'I can drive you wherever you want to go.'

'I think I'd better go just the same, Father,' she said with a smile, but he could have sworn she was fighting back tears. Something had gone wrong, dreadfully wrong, but he had no idea what it was and felt a complete fool.

'You'll keep in touch with me anyway?' he said.

'Indeed I will.'

'And if that fellow annoys you again, don't waste any more time. Come straight out of the shop and let me know. You understand that?'

'I promise, Father.'

Then she was gone and Fogarty felt let down. Let down, bewildered, frustrated, and he didn't know why. What her mother had said couldn't possibly have anything to do with it. It was advice that any mother might have given her daughter when she was leaving home for the first time, except for saying that 'all married men weren't like her daddy', which only showed the ingenuousness of the poor woman.

But why then had Sheila withered up when he referred to it, and above all, why had Joyce worn that complacent insolent smile when *he* referred to it? Then he understood and he withered up too. Sheila's mother had said something else, something about not throwing temptation in the way of priests because they were more vulnerable than other men. And quite innocently she had thrown temptation in his way and quite innocently he had been tempted, and Joyce in his coarse worldly way had seen it all. Her mother had known.

she was a lonely vulnerable girl and realized where it might carry her. And where it might have carried her – and him – God only knew, if he had not accidentally shown her how it all looked in an enemy's eye.

Now, Fogarty had a strong impression that he would never meet the girl again and never know what her mother had really said to her about not associating with a priest, because priests were weaker than other men, because they were more unprotected than other men. And suddenly the loneliness he was for ever trying to banish descended on him in all its black bitterness and he added aloud, 'O God, we are, we are!'

(1967)

THE CORKERYS

MAY MACMAHON was a good-looking girl, the only child of Jack MacMahon, the accountant, and his wife, Margaret. They lived in Cork, on Summerhill, the steep street that led from the flat of the city to the heights of Montenotte. She had always lived the life of a girl of good family, with piano lessons, dancing class, and crushes on her schoolfriends' brothers. Only occasionally did she wonder what it was all about, and then she invariably forgot to ask her father, who would certainly know. Her father knew everything, or almost everything. He was a tall, shy, good-looking man, who seemed to have been expecting martyrdom from his earliest years and drinking Irish whiskey to endure it. May's mother was small and pretty and very opinionated, though her opinions varied, and anyway did not last long. Her father's opinions never varied, and lasted for ever.

When May became friendly with the Corkery family, it turned out that he had always had strong opinions about them as well. Mr Corkery, a mild, inarticulate solicitor, whom May remembered going for lonely walks for the good of his health, had died and left his family with very limited means, but his widow had good connexions and managed to provide an education (mostly free) for all six children. Of the boys, the eldest, Tom, was now a Dominican, and, Joe who came next in line, was also going in for the priesthood. The Church was in the family's blood, because Mrs Corkery's brother was the Dean and her sister was Mother Superior of the convent of an enclosed order outside the city. Mrs Corkery's nickname among the children was

'Reverend Mother', and they accused her of imitating her sister, but Mrs Corkery only sniffed and said if everybody became priests and nuns there would soon be no Church left. Mrs Corkery seemed to believe quite seriously that the needs of the Church were the only possible excuse for sex.

From knowing the Corkerys May began to realize at last what life was about. It was no longer necessary to ask her father. Anyway he wouldn't know. He and her mother were nice but commonplace. Everything they said and did was dull and predictable, and even when they went to Mass on Sunday they did so only because everyone else did it. The Corkerys were rarely dull and never predictable. Though their whole life seemed to centre on the Church, they were not in the least pietistic. The Dean fought with Mrs Corkery; Father Tim fought with Joe; the sisters fought with their brothers, who, they said, were getting all the attention, and fought one another when their brothers were not available. Tessie, the eldest girl, known as 'The Limb of the Devil', or just 'The Limb', was keeping company with a young stockbroker who told her a lot of dirty stories, which she repeated with great gusto to her brothers, particularly to Father Tim. This, however, was for family reasons, because they all agreed that Tim was inclined to put on airs.

And then The Limb astonished everybody by entering the convent where her aunt was Mother Superior. May attended the Reception in the little convent chapel, which struck her to the heart by its combination of poverty and gentility. She felt that the ceremony might have been tolerable in a great cathedral with a choir and thundering organ, but not in that converted drawing-room, where the nuns knelt along the side walls and squeaked like mourners. The Limb was laid out on the altar and first covered with roses as though she were dead; then an old nun clipped her long black hair with a shears. It fell and lay at her head as though it too had died. May drew a quick breath and glanced at Joe, who was kneeling beside her. Though he had his hands over his face, she knew from the way his shoulders moved that he was crying. Then she cried, too.

For a full week the ceremony gave her the horrors every time she remembered it, and she felt she should have nothing more to do with such an extraordinary family. All the same, a week with her parents was enough to make her realize the attraction of the Corkerys even more than before.

'Did it scare you, May?' Rosie, the second girl, asked with a wicked grin. 'Cripes, it put the fear of God into me. I'm not having any of that *de profundis* stuff; I'm joining a decent missionary order.' This was the first May had heard of Rosie's vocation. Inside a year, she, too, was in a convent, but in Rome, and 'having a gas time', as she casually reported home.

They really were an extraordinary family, and the Dean was as queer as any of them. The Sunday following the ceremony May was at dinner there, and he put his hand firmly on her shoulder as though he were about to yank off her dress, and gave her a crooked smile that would have convinced any reasonable observer that he was a sex maniac, and yet May knew that almost every waking moment his thoughts were concentrated on outwitting the Bishop, who seemed to be the greatest enemy of the Church since Nero. The Bishop was a Dominican, and the Dean felt that a monk's place was in the cloister.

'The man is a bully!' he said, with an astonishment and grief that would have moved any audience but his own family.

'Oh, now, Mick!' said Mrs Corkery placidly. She was accustomed to hearing the Bishop denounced.

'I'm sorry, Josephine,' the Dean said with a formal regret that rang equally untrue. 'The man is a bully. An infernal bully, what's more. I'm not criticizing you or the order, Tim,' he said, looking at his nephew over his spectacles, 'but monks simply have no place in ecclesiastical affairs. Let them stick to their prayers is what I say.'

'And a queer way the world would be only for them,' Joe

said. Joe was going for the secular priesthood himself, but he didn't like to see his overwhelming uncle get away with too much.

'Their influence on Church history has been disastrous!' the Dean bellowed, reaching for his cigarette case. 'Always, or almost always, disastrous. That man thinks he knows everything.'

'Maybe he does,' said Joe.

'Maybe,' said the Dean, like an old bull who cannot ignore a dart from any quarter. 'But as well as that, he interferes in everything, and always publicly, always with the greatest possible amount of scandal. "I don't like the model of that church"; "Take away that statue"; "That painting is irreverent". Begob, Joe, I don't think even you know as much as that. I declare to God, Josephine, I believe if anyone suggested it to him that man would start inspecting the cut of the schoolgirls' panties.' And when everyone roared with laughter, the Dean raised his head sternly and said, 'I mean it.'

Peter, the youngest boy, never got involved in these family arguments about the Bishop, the orders, or the future of the Church. He was the odd man out. He was apprenticed in his father's old firm and would grow up to be owner or partner. In every Irish family there is a boy like Peter whose task it is to take on the family responsibilities. It was merely an accident that he was the youngest. What counted was that he was his mother's favourite. Even before he had a mind to make up, he knew it was not for him to become too involved, because someone would have to look after his mother in her old age. He might marry, but it would have to be a wife who suited her. He was the ugliest of the children, though with a monkey ugliness that was almost as attractive as Father Tim's film-star looks and Joe's ascetic masculine fire. He was slow, watchful, and good-humoured, with high cheekbones that grew tiny bushes of hair, and he had a lazy malice that could often be as effective as the uproarious indignation of his brothers and sisters.

May, who saw the part he had been cast for, wondered whether she couldn't woo Mrs Corkery as well as another girl.

After Rosie there was Joe, who was ordained the following year, and then Sheela did what seemed – in that family, at least – the conventional thing and went into the same convent as Tessie.

It was an extraordinary family, and May was never quite able to understand the fascination it had for her. Partly, of course – and this she felt rather than understood – it was the attraction of the large family for the only child, the sheer relief of never having to wonder what you were going to play next. But beside this there was an attraction rather like that of a large theatrical family – the feeling that everything was related to a larger imaginative world. In a sense, the Corkerys always seemed to be playing.

She knew that her own being in love with Peter was part of her love affair with the family as a whole, the longing to be connected with them, and the teasing she got about Peter from his brothers and sisters suggested that they, too, recognized it and were willing to accept her as one of themselves. But she also saw that her chance of ever marrying Peter was extremely slight, because Peter was not attracted by her. When he could have been out walking with her he was out walking with his friend Mick MacDonald, and when the pair of them came in while she was in the house, Peter behaved to her as though she were nothing more than a welcome stranger. He was always polite, always deferential – unlike Tim and Joe, who treated her as though she were an extra sister, to be slapped on the bottom or pushed out of the way as the mood struck them.

May was a serious girl; she had read books on modern psychology, and she knew that the very quality that made Peter settle for a life in the world made him unsuitable as a husband. It was strange how right the books were about that. He was dominated by his mother, and he could flirt with her as he never flirted with May. Clearly, no other woman would ever entirely replace his mother in his heart. In fact (May was too serious a girl not to give things their proper names), Peter was the very type of the homosexual – the latent homosexual, as she learned to call it.

Other boys *wanted* to go out with her, and she resented Peter's unfailing courtesy, though in more philosophic spells she realized that he probably couldn't help it, and that when he showed his almost boyish hero-worship of Mick Mac-Donald before her it was not his fault but Nature's. All the same, she thought it very uncalled-for on the part of Nature, because it left her no particular interest in a world in which the only eligible young man was a queer. After a year or two of this, her thoughts turned more and more to the quiet convent where the Corkery girls contentedly carried on their simple lives of meditation and prayer. Once or twice she dropped a dark hint that she was thinking of becoming a nun herself, but each time it led to a scene with her father.

'You're a fool, girl!' he said harshly, getting up to pour himself an extra drink. May knew he didn't altogether resent being provoked, because it made him feel entitled to drink more.

'Now, Jack, you must not say things like that,' her mother said anxiously.

'Of course I have to say it. Look at her! At her age! And she doesn't even have a boy!'

'But if there isn't a boy who interests her!'

'There are plenty of boys who'd interest her if only she behaved like a natural girl,' he said gloomily. 'What do you think a boy wants to do with a girl? Say the rosary? She hasn't behaved naturally ever since she got friendly with that family – what's their name?'

'Corkery,' Mrs MacMahon said, having failed to perceive that not remembering the Corkerys' name was the one way the poor man had of getting back at them.

'Whatever their name is, they've turned her into an idiot. That's no great surprise. They never had any brains to distribute, themselves.'

'But still, Jack, you will admit they've got on very well.'

'They've got on very well!' he echoed scornfully. 'In the Church! Except that young fellow, the solicitor's clerk, and I suppose he hadn't brains enough even for the Church. They should have put him in the friars.'

'But after all, their uncle is the Dean.'

'Wonderful Dean, too,' grumbled Jack MacMahon. 'He drove me out of twelve-o'clock Mass, so as not to listen to his drivel. He can hardly speak decent English, not to mind preaching a sermon. "A bunch of baloney!" ' he quoted angrily. 'If we had a proper bishop, instead of the one we have, he'd make that fellow speak correctly in the pulpit at least.'

'But it's only so that his congregation will understand him, Jack.'

'Oh, his congregation understands him only too well. Himself and his tall hat and his puffed-up airs! Common, that's what he is, and that's what all the family are, on both sides. If your daughter wants to be a nun, you and the Corkerys can arrange it between you. But not one penny of my money goes into their pockets, believe me!'

May was sorry to upset him, but for herself she did not mind his loathing of the whole Corkery family. She knew that it was only because he was fond of her and dreaded being left without her in his old age. He had spoiled her so long as she was not of an age to answer him back, and she guessed he was looking forward to spoiling his grandchildren even worse because he would not live long enough to hear them answer him back. But this, she realized, was what the Corkerys had done for her – made all that side of life seem unimportant.

She had a long talk with Mother Agatha, Mrs Corkery's sister, about her vocation, which confirmed her in her resolution. Mother Agatha was very unlike her sister, who was loud-voiced and humorous. The Mother Superior was pale, thin, cool, and with the slightest trace of an ironic wit that might have passed unnoticed by a stupider girl. But May noticed it, and realized that she was being observed very closely indeed.

She and her mother did the shopping for the trousseau, but the bills and parcels were kept carefully out of her father's sight. Drunk or sober, he refused to discuss the matter at all. 'It would only upset him just now, poor man,' her mother said philosophically. He was drinking heavily, and when he was in liquor he quarrelled a lot with her mother about little things. With May he avoided quarrels, or even arguments, and it struck her that he was training himself for a life in which he would no longer have her to quarrel with. On the day of the Reception he did not drink at all, which pleased her, and was icily polite to everybody, but when, later, she appeared behind the parlour grille, all in white, and the sun caught her, she saw his face in the darkness of the parlour, with all the life drained out of it, and suddenly he turned and left without a word. It was only then that a real feeling of guilt sprang up in her at the thought of the miserable old age that awaited him – a man like him, who loved young creatures who could not answer him back, and who would explain to them unweariedly about the sun and moon and geography and figures. She had answered him back in a way that left him with nothing to look forward to.

All the same, there was something very comforting about the life of an enclosed order. It had been organized a long, long time before, by people who knew more about the intrusions of the outside world than May did. The panics that had seized her about her ability to sustain the life diminished and finally ceased. The round of duties, services, and mortifications was exactly what she had needed, and little by little she felt, the last traces of worldliness slip from her – even the very human worry about the old age of her father and mother. The convent was poor, and not altogether from choice. Everything in the house was mean and clean and cheerful, and May grew to love the old drawing-room that had been turned into a chapel, where she knelt in her own place, through the black winter mornings when at home she would still be tucked up comfortably in bed. She liked the rough feeling of her clothes and the cold of the floor through her sandals, though mostly she liked the proximity of Tessie and Sheela.

There were times when, reading the lives of the saints, she wished she had lived in more heroic times, and she secretly invented minor mortifications for herself to make sure she could endure them. It was not until she had been in the convent for close on a year that she noticed that the minor mortifications were liable to be followed by major depressions. Though she was a clever woman, she did not try to analyse this. She merely lay awake at night and realized that the nuns she lived with – even Tessie and Sheela – were not the stuff of saints and martyrs, but ordinary women who behaved in religion very much as they would have behaved in marriage, and who followed the rule in the spirit in which her father went to Mass on Sundays. There was nothing whatever to be said against them, and any man who had got one of them for a wife would probably have considered himself fortunate, but all the same there was something about them that was not quite grown-up. It was very peculiar and caused her great concern. The things that had really frightened her about the order when she was in the world – the loneliness, the austerity, the ruthless discipline – now seemed to her meaningless and harmless. After that she saw with horror that the great days of the Church were over, and that they were merely a lot of perfectly commonplace women play-acting austerity and meditation.

'But my dear child,' Mother Agatha said when May wept out her story to her, 'of course we're only children. Of course we're only play-acting. How else does a child learn obedience and discipline?'

And when May talked to her about what the order had been in earlier days, that vague, ironic note crept into Mother Superior's voice, as though she had heard it all many times before. 'I know, Sister,' she said, with a nod. 'Believe me, I do know that the order was stricter in earlier times. But you must remember that it was not founded in a semi-arctic climate like ours, so there was less chance of the sisters dying of double pneumonia. I have talked to half the plumbers in town, but it seems that central heating is not understood here . . . everything is relative. I'm sure we suffer just as much in our very comfortable sandals as the early sisters suffered in their bare feet, and probably at times rather more, but at any rate we are not here for the sole purpose of suffering mortification, whatever pleasures it may hold for us.'

Every word Mother Agatha said made perfect sense to May while she was saying it, and May knew she was being ungrateful and hysterical, but when the interview was over and the sound of her sobs had died away, she was left with the impression that Mother Agatha was only another commonplace woman, with a cool manner and a sarcastic tongue, who was also acting the part of a nun. She was alone in a world of bad actors and actresses, and the Catholicism she had known and believed in was dead.

A few weeks later she was taken to a private nursing home. 'Just for a short rest, Sister,' as Mother Agatha said. 'It's a very pleasant place, and you will find a lot of other Religious there who need a rest as well.'

There followed an endless but timeless phase of weeping and confusion, when all May's ordinary life was broken up and strange men burst into her room and examined her and asked questions she did not understand and replied to questions of hers in a way that showed they had not understood them either. Nobody seemed to realize that she was the last Catholic in the world; nobody understood her tears about it. Above all, nobody seemed to be able to hear the gramophone record that played continuously in her head, and that stopped only when they gave her an injection.

Then, one spring day, she went into the garden for a walk and a young nurse saw her back to her room. Far ahead of them, at the other end of a long, white corridor, she saw an old man with his back to her, and remembered that she had seen his face many times before and had perceived, without paying attention to, his long, gloomy, ironic face. She knew she must have remembered him, because now she could see nothing but his back, and suddenly the words 'Who is that queer old man?' broke through the sound of the gramophone record, surprising her as much as they seemed to surprise the young nurse.

'Oh, him!' the nurse said, with a smile. 'Don't you know him? He's been here for years.'

'But why, Nurse?'

'Oh, he doesn't think he's a priest, and he is one really, that's the trouble.'

'But how extraordinary!'

'Isn't it?' the nurse said, biting her lower lip in a smile. 'Cripes, you'd think 'twas something you wouldn't forget. He's nice, really, though,' she added gravely, as though she felt she had been criticizing him.

When they reached Mary's room, the young nurse grinned again, in a guilty way, and May noticed that she was extravagantly pretty, with small gleaming front teeth.

'*You're* getting all right, anyway,' she said.

'Oh, really?' May said vaguely, because she knew she was not getting all right. 'Why do you think that, Nurse?'

'Oh, you get to spot things,' the nurse said with a shrug, and left May uncomforted, because she didn't know if she really did get well how she could face the convent and the other nuns again. All of them, she felt, would be laughing at her. Instead of worrying about the nuns, she went into a mournful daydream about the old priest who did not think he was a priest, and next day, when her father called, she said intensely, 'Daddy, there's a priest in here who doesn't believe he's a priest – isn't that extraordinary?' She did not hear the tone of her own voice or know how reasonable it sounded, and so she was surprised when her father looked away and started fumbling mechanically in his jacket pocket for a cigarette.

'Well, you don't have to think you're a nun either,' he said, with an unsteady voice. 'Your mother has your own room ready for you when you come home.'

'Oh, but Daddy, I have to go back to the convent.'

'Oh, no you don't. No more convents for you, young lady! That's fixed up already with Mother Superior. It was all a mistake from the beginning. You're coming straight home to your mother and me.'

Then May knew she was really going to get well, and she wanted to go home with him at once, not to go back up the stairs behind the big iron door where there was always an attendant on duty. She knew that going back home meant defeat, humiliation, and despair, but she no longer cared even about that. She just wanted to take up her life again at the point where it had gone wrong, when she had first met the Corkerys.

Her father brought her home and acted as though he had rescued her from a dragon's den. Each evening, when he came home from work, he sat with her, sipping at his drink and talking quietly and comfortably. She felt he was making great efforts to assure that she felt protected and relaxed. Most of the time she did, but there were spells when she wanted her mother to put her back in the nursing home.

'Oh, I couldn't do that,' her mother said characteristically. 'It would upset your poor father too much.'

But she did discuss it with the doctor – a young man, thin and rather unhealthy-looking, who looked as though he, too, was living on his nerves – and he argued with May about it.

'But what am I to do, Doctor, when I feel like this?' she asked plaintively.

'Go out and get jarred,' he said briskly.

'Get what, Doctor?' she asked feebly.

'Jarred,' he repeated without embarrassment. 'Stoned. Polluted. Drunk. I don't mean alone, of course. You need a young fellow along with you.'

'Oh, not that again, Doctor!' she said, and for some reason her voice came out exactly like Mother Agatha's – which was not how she intended it to sound.

'And some sort of a job,' he went on remorselessly. 'There isn't a damn thing wrong with you except that you think you're a failure. You're not, of course, but as a result of thinking you are you've scratched the surface of your mind all over, and when you sit here like this, looking out at the rain, you keep rubbing it so that it doesn't heal. Booze, love-making, and hard work – they keep your hands away from the sore surface, and then it heals of its own accord.'

She did her best, but it didn't seem to heal as easily as all that. Her father got her a job in the office of a friend, and she listened, in fascination, to the chatter of the other secretaries. She even went out in the evening with a couple of them and listened to their common little love stories. She knew if she had to wait until she talked like that about fellows in order to be well, her case was hopeless. Instead, she got drunk and told them how she had been for years in love with a homosexual, and, as she told it, the story became so hopeless and dreadful that she sobbed over it herself. After that she went home and wept for hours, because she knew that she had been telling lies, and betrayed the only people in the world whom she had really cared for.

Her father made a point of never referring at all to the Corkerys, the convent, or the nursing home. She knew that for him this represented a real triumph of character, because he loathed the Corkerys more than ever for what he believed they had done to her. But even he could not very well ignore the latest development in the saga. It seemed that Mrs Corkery herself had decided to become a nun. She announced placidly to everyone that she had done her duty by her family, who were now all comfortably settled, and that she felt free to do what she had always wanted to do anyhow. She discussed it with the Dean, who practically excommunicated her on the spot. He said the family would never live down the scandal, and Mrs Corkery told him it wasn't the scandal that worried him at all but the loss of the one house where he could get a decent meal. If he had a spark of manliness, she said, he would get rid of his housekeeper, who couldn't cook, was a miserable sloven, and ordered him about as if he were a schoolboy. The Dean said she would have to get permission in writing from every one of her children, and Mrs Corkery replied calmly that there was no difficulty whatever about that.

May's father didn't really want to crow, but he could not resist pointing out that he had always said the Corkerys had a slate loose.

'I don't see anything very queer about it,' May said stubbornly.

'A woman with six children entering a convent at her age!' her father said, not even troubling to grow angry with her. 'Even the Dean realizes it's mad.'

'It *is* a little bit extreme, all right,' her mother said, with a frown, but May knew she was thinking of her.

May had the feeling that Mrs Corkery would make a very good nun, if for no other reason than to put her brother and Mother Agatha in their place. And of course, there were other reasons. As a girl she had wanted to be a nun, but for family reasons it was impossible, so she had become a good wife and mother, instead. Now, after thirty years of pinching and scraping, her family had grown away from her and she could return to her early dream. There was nothing unbalanced about that, May thought bitterly. *She* was the one who had proved unbalanced.

For a while it plunged her back into gloomy moods, and they were made worse by the scraps of gossip that people passed on to her, not knowing how they hurt. Mrs Corkery had collected her six letters of freedom and taken them herself to the Bishop, who had immediately given in. 'Spite!' the Dean pronounced gloomily. 'Nothing but spite – all because I don't support his mad dream of turning a modern city into a medieval monastery.'

On the day of Mrs Corkery's Reception, May did not leave the house at all. It rained, and she sat by the sitting-room window, looking across the city to where the hills were almost invisible. She was living Mrs Corkery's day through – the last day in the human world of an old woman who had assumed the burden she herself had been too weak to accept. She could see it all as though she were back in that mean, bright little chapel, with the old woman lying out on the altar, covered with roses like a corpse, and an old nun shearing off her thin grey locks. It was all so intolerably vivid that May kept bursting into sudden fits of tears and whimpering like a child.

One evening a few weeks later, she came out of the office in the rain and saw Peter Corkery at the other side of the street. She obeyed her first instinct and bowed her head so as not to look at him. Her heart sank as he crossed the road to accost her.

'Aren't you a great stranger, May?' he asked, with his cheerful grin.

'We're very busy in the office these days, Peter,' she replied, with false brightness.

'It was only the other night Joe was talking about you. You know Joe is up in the seminary now?'

'No. What's he doing?'

'Teaching. He finds it a great relief after the mountains. And, of course, you know about the mother.' This was it!

'I heard about it. I suppose ye're all delighted?'

'*I* wasn't very delighted,' he said, and his lips twisted in pain. ' 'Twas the most awful day I ever spent. When they cut off her hair—'

'You don't have to remind me.'

'I disgraced myself, May. I had to run out of the chapel.

And here I had two nuns after me, trying to steer me to the lavatory. Why do nuns always think a man is looking for a lavatory?'

'I wouldn't know. I wasn't a very good one.'

'There are different opinions about that,' he said gently, but he only hurt her more.

'And I suppose you'll be next?'

'How next?'

'I was sure you had a vocation, too.'

'I don't know,' he said thoughtfully. 'I never really asked myself. I suppose, in a way, it depends on you.'

'And what have I to say to it?' she asked in a ladylike tone, though her heart suddenly began to pant.

'Only whether you're going to marry me or not. Now I have the house to myself and only Mrs Maher looking after me. You remember Mrs Maher?'

'And you think I'd make a cheap substitute for Mrs Maher, I suppose?' she asked, and suddenly all the pent-up anger and frustration of years seemed to explode inside her. She realized that it was entirely because of him that she had become a nun, because of him she had been locked up in a nursing home and lived the life of an emotional cripple. 'Don't you think that's an extraordinary sort of proposal – if it's intended to be a proposal.'

'Why the hell should I be any good at proposing? How many girls do you think I've proposed to?'

'Not many, since they didn't teach you better manners. And it would never occur to yourself to say you loved me. Do you?' she almost shouted. 'Do you love me?'

'Sure, of course I do,' he said, almost in astonishment. 'I wouldn't be asking you to marry me otherwise. But all the same—'

'All the same, all the same, you have reservations!' And suddenly language that would have appalled her to hear a few months before broke from her, before she burst into uncontrollable tears and went running homeward through the rain. 'God damn you to Hell, Peter Corkery! I wasted my life on you, and now in the heel of the hunt all you can say to me is "All the same". You'd better go back to your damn pansy pals, and say it to them.'

She was hysterical by the time she reached Summerhill. Her father's behaviour was completely characteristic. He was the born martyr and this was only another of the ordeals for which he had been preparing himself all his life. He got up and poured himself a drink.

'Well, there is one thing I'd better tell you now, daughter,' he said quietly but firmly. 'That man will never enter this house in my lifetime.'

'Oh, nonsense, Jack MacMahon!' his wife said in a rage, and she went and poured herself a drink, a thing she did under her husband's eye only when she was prepared to fling it at him. 'You haven't a scrap of sense. Don't you see now that the boy's mother only entered the convent because she knew he'd never feel free while she was in the world?'

'Oh, Mother!' May cried, startled out of her hysterics.

'Well, am I right?' her mother said, drawing herself up.

'Oh, you're right, you're right,' May said, beginning to sob again. 'Only I was such a fool it never occurred to me. Of course, she was doing it for me.'

'And for her son,' said her mother. 'And if he's anything like his mother, I'll be very proud to claim him for a son-in-law.'

She looked at her husband, but saw that she had made her effect and could now enjoy her drink in peace. 'Of course, in some ways it's going to be very embarrassing,' she went on peaceably. 'We can't very well say, "Mr Peter Corkery, son of Sister Rosina of the Little Flower" or whatever the dear lady's name is. In fact, it's very difficult to see how we're going to get it into the Press at all. However, as I always say, if the worst comes to the worst, there's a lot to be said for a quiet wedding . . . I do hope you were nice to him, May?' she asked.

It was only then that May remembered that she hadn't been in the least nice, and in fact, had used language that would have horrified her mother. Not that it would make much difference. She and Peter had travelled so far together, and by such extraordinary ways.

(1966)

THE SCHOOL FOR WIVES

THE real trouble with love is that people want contradictory things out of it. Like Jimmy Maguire and his wife. Jimmy was a tall thin fellow with an eager face, and in his younger days he used to be something of a Don Juan. There was a little group of them – the Doctor, Con Bishop, and two or three other bachelors – and they were all out for a good time. They used to go shooting and fishing, and one year, I remember, they took a house in Clare. The things that went on! Any excuse for a party, and it didn't much matter to them where the party was to be – Limerick, Galway, or Cork, what was it, after all, but a day's outing? Jimmy was the most reckless of them. They would be returning to Dublin from one outing when he would hear of a party somewhere else, and decide they ought to crash it. The Doctor, who shared a flat with Jimmy, lived in a continual state of alarm at what Jimmy would do next. Jimmy would do anything if the mood struck him, and, whatever he did, the Doctor was swept protesting into his orbit.

'But it's all right,' Jimmy would say, raising a hand. 'The man is an old friend. I've done business with him for years.'

'Business?' the Doctor would say. 'You don't even know his name.'

'Oh, what's a little thing like that between friends?'

And Jimmy would go up to the house of a perfect stranger and brazen it out. You wouldn't think from his rather formal manners that he was so audacious, but he was. And he could get away with things, for he was personable and plausible. Not only would he gain admittance to the party, he would end by becoming the centre of it. The secret of Jimmy's success was his fondness for women. He really liked women, and had a quite genuine interest in their affairs, and a woman could never be with him for long without telling him her troubles. Whatever wonderful way he had of easing their minds, women who confessed to him wanted to go on confessing, and that was where the Doctor came in, because he would talk to them over the telephone in that wonderful, vague, syrupy voice of his, sympathizing with them in their inability to find Jimmy, while Jimmy in stockinged feet tiptoed around him, making hideous faces.

All this greatly scandalized the Doctor. But for all his alarm and pretended disapproval he loved it, of course. He had been devoted to his mother and, as a result, he was still unmarried and likely to remain so. Jimmy was his secret life, his wild oats. He was lonely and sweet-natured and for ever thinking and talking of love. You would go to see him, and he would fuss about with the drinks, murmuring in his gentle, worried way about Jimmy and his girls. 'And some of them married, my dear fellow,' he would whisper, giving you a dark look over his spectacles. 'I forget whether you like soda. Personally, I think it gives you indigestion. And he's so pious! Every year of his life off to Lough Derg on the pilgrimage, trailing round the holy stones on his bare feet. And even there – did I put too much water in it – he picks them up. At the same time – here's health, old man – he keeps trying to reform me. I admit my beliefs mightn't be all that orthodox, but I can't help feeling that his aren't completely sincere. Mind you, he's quite charming about it. He says I'm putting the cart before the horse, and that sins against morals are less important than sins against faith. According to him, I'm a Protestant. He says it's all in the importance you attach to the First Commandment, or something. I really can't follow that sort of argument – I mean, this difference between sins against faith and sins against morals. Can you?'

At last, after years of piety and skirt-hunting, Jimmy found the girl he wanted to marry, and he took her by storm. She was called Roisin Mooney, and I must say he showed great taste. She was a really nice girl, the sort you'd swear would be especially reserved as a reward for virtue. She was enraptured with religion, with the sacraments, with prayer, and with every form of emotional religion. Nor did marriage seem to disillusion her. At least twenty times a day that girl must have told herself that she was the luckiest girl in the world to be married to a king of men like Jimmy, and twenty times a day wondered if God would give her the grace to be worthy of him. It is the unworldly type of woman whose mind is fixed on the saints, suffering, and sublimation who really appreciates the miracle of a man in the bed when she wakes in the morning.

She asked him over and over to explain again from the beginning what he had felt when he first met her and how it was he had seen anything in such a plain, stupid, uneducated girl as herself. And Jimmy, who found it difficult to remember even where he had met her and whose approach to all women had been standardized down the years, tried to look portentous and understanding, and said that a legal training was a great aid in seeing through appearances. Roisin shook her head doubtfully. She had known other lawyers, and they had never seen through her. Clearly it couldn't be anything but inspiration, and she worried her own vivid recollections, trying to see portents and miracles in them, but she couldn't, because, as she recognized herself, she wasn't clever.

Jimmy had a rajah's life with her. To say that Roisin was a good housekeeper would be an absurdity. She kept house for him as a musician writes a symphony or a saint pursues a meditation – on her knees, in quest of the absolute. When he got home from the office, she knelt at his feet and took off his shoes, while Jimmy made faces to indicate the various inconsiderate ways in which she hurt his feet. When she had got him a drink and asked him for the tenth time if it was all right, she sat on a little stool and looked up adoringly at him while that scoundrel pontificated. And when he came home drunk and climbed into bed, with his bowler hat down over his eyes and his umbrella resting neatly on his left arm, she gently relieved him of both, took off his shoes and socks, opened his collar and tie, and crept into bed beside him, thanking God for the gift of a wonderful husband. She was a real pet.

Those who had known Jimmy in his bachelor days wondered how long exactly it would take him to grow tired of living with a saint and long for the open road again and the wild parties in Galway and Cork. But that was not how it happened at all. Instead, Jimmy began to drop all his old friends, the Doctor among them. He didn't do it blatantly or rudely, because, whatever faults Jimmy may have had, he was a thorough gentleman. But he dropped them just the same. Occasionally the Doctor would run into him in Dame Street, coming from his office, and Jimmy's face would light up, and the pair of them would drop into the Wicklow Bar or Davy Byrne's, while Jimmy sketched the wonderful party he was going to give for all his old friends, till that glazed look came in his eye and he had to go home in a cab.

But the Doctor noticed that no matter how glazed Jimmy's eyes got, the invitation never became more precise.

'Jimmy,' he said dryly, 'I don't want to be offensive or personal in any way, but if you'd put a tenth of the energy into giving that party that you put into talking about it, we might have some chance of attending it before we die.'

'Next week definitely Pat,' said Jimmy, drawing himself up with a frown. 'Thursday or Friday, depending. I'll ring you.'

But the next week came and he didn't ring, and there was no party. The Doctor was hurt. He realized that Jimmy was dropping the old crowd for business acquaintances, clients, and priests. Particularly priests. A man who is trying to exorcize his past can't do better than priests. Now when he got a bit high, Jimmy talked about the Dialogue Mass instead of ankles, or the difference between ourselves and the Greek Orthodox Church. He took Roisin to the pictures, wearing the impeccable bowler hat and carrying the umbrella. Jimmy was on the way up. In no time now he would be solicitor to half a dozen government agencies.

Jimmy's old friends couldn't help being curious about the eager, dark-haired girl he had married, but what they didn't know was that Roisin was even more curious about them. Marriage was still wonderful. She was having a baby, and she lit candles to Jimmy, she was full of Jimmy, but none of the people he brought to the house really knew Jimmy. When Roisin had one drink in – one drink was always enough to loosen her tongue – she had to tell the whole amazing story of Jimmy's courtship. 'And do you know how that fellow proposed to me?' she would say. 'He made me sit on the side of the road and then took out his handkerchief and *knelt* in front of me as if I was a statue. "Jimmy Maguire!" says I. "Get up out of that or you'll ruin your new trousers." '

But when she looked at their polite, vague, smiling faces, she had the feeling that they only thought her a fool. And in the middle of the night she woke Jimmy to ask him to tell her frankly whether she hadn't ruined his life. Jimmy yawned and said no, she was doing fine.

'But I want to know the truth. I'd sooner know it now when I might be able to do something about it,' she would say, as if she were begging the specialist to hold nothing back from her. 'I do my best, but I know I haven't the brains. I was always the same. I never could do sums. No wonder if they think I'm mad.'

And all the time at the back of Roisin's mind was the thought that the person who would really understand her was Josephine Hanrahan. She knew that Jimmy and Josephine Hanrahan had been very thick. She did not know in which way, nor did she very much care, but she was certain that a woman who had been so fond of Jimmy would understand her feelings. This was where the first rift occurred between Jimmy and herself, for Jimmy did not like the idea at all. Not that he showed how troubled he really was. Instead, he pretended to consider the matter judicially.

'Now, Josephine is a delightful woman,' he said in a harsh tone, 'but she isn't your class. Please don't think I'm being snobbish. There's nothing I dislike more. But we have to face facts, and it wouldn't be in the woman's best interests.'

To sacrifice a pleasure in order to spare pain to Josephine appealed immensely to Roisin's idealistic mind, but all the same she couldn't help wondering if it was really necessary. And Jimmy, in his quiet Machiavellian way, fed her another curate, who kept her quiet for a few months, till she started to wonder what sort of man the Doctor was.

'Well, Paddy is a fellow you might find interesting,' Jimmy said thoughtfully, filling his pipe. 'As a study, that is. But unfortunately the way we're situated we can't very well ask him to the house. You see, Paddy is an atheist.'

'An atheist?' Roisin said, brightening up at once. She had never met an atheist. 'You never told me that.'

'Ah, well, it's not right to say things like that about your friends,' Jimmy said loyally. 'But he might just make an offensive remark in front of poor Father Joe that would upset him.'

Of course it was a slander; the Doctor was incapable of being offensive to anybody, but Roisin didn't know this and had to rest content with the excuse. Then, after racking his brains, Jimmy dug up some old businessman who had painted watercolours in his youth and had known everybody; one night when he was drunk Yeats had brought him home. But his conversation with Yeats seemed to have been of much the same kind as his conversation with Roisin. By this time, Little Liam was born, and for quite a while Roisin's attention was diverted from everything else in the world. Except that even then she was slipping out to the

optician's wife next door for a cup of tea or a glass of sherry
– anything to escape the curates. The optician's wife was a
shrewd, interfering woman. She didn't know what Jimmy
was up to, but she knew Jimmy was trying to keep his wife
to himself, and that was enough for her.

One evening the Doctor was sitting in the lounge of the
Wicklow Hotel with Jimmy when Josephine Hanrahan
looked in. The Doctor, who was very polite and very fond of
her, jumped to his feet and signalled to her.

'Don't bother to get up, Paddy,' she said. 'I'm not staying.
If I'm not good enough to drink with a man in his own
house, I see no reason for doing it in public.'

'Oh, really, Josephine!' Jimmy protested.

'I didn't think you'd do it, Jimmy,' she said bitterly. 'I
really didn't. I thought you were too big a man to drop your
old friends.'

Jimmy looked owlishly at the Doctor, then at her, and
held out his hands. 'Do I look like a man who's dropped his
old friends?' he asked triumphantly.

'Oh, you're too clever for that, Jimmy,' she replied. 'You're
not obvious. But you won't ask us to your house, and you
won't let us meet your wife. Has Paddy been there?'

'No, dear,' the Doctor said, trying to make his voice sound
smooth. 'Are you sure you won't have a drink?'

'Quite, Paddy,' she said. But she was not to be shut up. She
turned on Jimmy again. 'But you'll invite people who never
spoke to you a year ago and wouldn't speak to you
tomorrow if you hadn't money in your pocket.'

Jimmy took his glasses off and wiped his long, pale face as
though to reveal the true features below. The character he
was trying to assume now was the haggard, patient, over-
worked family man, and to give him his due he did it well.
'My dear girl,' he said kindly, wagging his glasses at her, 'in
my business I have to entertain people I don't much care
for.' He stopped and picked up the bowler hat. 'This is a
façade. And you know it.'

'Lies, Jimmy Maguire!' she said in a whisper. 'I know your

faults. I probably know them better than you do yourself. But you're not mean, and you're not calculating and you're not avaricious.'

He drew himself up, smiled, and raised the bowler to her, 'Thank you, my dear.'

'You didn't let me finish,' she went on. 'I never said you weren't jealous.'

'Jealous?' he echoed as though he didn't know what she meant.

'Yes, jealous.'

'But of whom, Josephine?' Jimmy said, with an elaboration of astonishment that did not seem genuine.

'Of your wife.'

'That shows all you know about Roisin.'

'No, that shows all you know about her. You're afraid she'll do what other wives have done – wives well known to you.'

The Doctor didn't know where to look. Jimmy didn't like it either. 'Really, Josephine,' he said, 'that's pretty far-fetched, even from you.'

'You never made a bigger mistake in your life, Jimmy Maguire,' she said contemptuously. 'And you'll regret it.'

'Extraordinary ideas women get into their heads,' Jimmy said when she had gone. 'I hope that husband isn't giving her more trouble.'

The Doctor could see he was disturbed. That evening he did not reach the glazing stage, and they separated at the bus stop by Trinity College. The Doctor went away feeling thoughtful. For he, too, had been to the optician's house and wondered afterwards why on earth he had been invited and why the optician's wife had pressed him to come again. He began to feel that he was involved in an intrigue.

The next time he went there, he saw Con Bishop in a corner, and then he knew that he was right. Con was another of the old group. He was an architect, an excitable young man with an Oxford accent. He flirted with the optician's wife as he flirted with everybody. The Doctor was sitting with another medical man, drinking his whiskey, when the door opened and Roisin Maguire came in. Ignoring everyone else, she went straight up to the Doctor and took his hands in hers and dragged him over to the sofa.

'I'm always wanting to talk to you,' she exclaimed intensely, gazing into his eyes.

'It's mutual,' he said, never having seen a technique like this before – if it was a technique, which he couldn't be sure of. 'But I don't see as much of Jimmy as I used to.'

'Ah, who does?' she said in a husky voice. 'You can't see him for curates. I love my religion – you probably think I don't, but I do – only I can't bear too many priests round the house. Maybe I shouldn't say it to you, but I can't help it.'

'Why on earth shouldn't you say it?' asked the Doctor, overwhelmed by her manner.

'I shouldn't – not to an atheist.'

The Doctor was on the point of asking who had told her this when their hostess, who felt this was all much too sudden and public, descended on them. Still Roisin did not let go of the Doctor's hands. Instead, she looked over her shoulder at Mrs Lacey and said, 'Ah, Kitty, haven't I waited long enough for a chance to talk to this fellow? Be a sport and bring me an old drink. Anything at all will do. It all has the same effect on me ... Aren't I awful?' she asked the Doctor. 'I can never tell the difference between one drink and another.' But her mind was not on the drink any more than it was on the party. She had a sort of rapt, entranced quality, as though she were a sleepwalker living out a dream. 'Tell me, aren't you the one that bailed Jimmy out when he was arrested in Limerick?'

'No,' the Doctor said with amusement. 'I'm afraid that was Con, the fair-haired chap over there.'

'I want to talk to him, too,' she said, squeezing the Doctor's hands. 'I'm always hearing about ye. And there was a woman in the car with him the same night, wasn't there? He won't tell me who she was. That fellow is the devil. Do you know was it Josephine Hanrahan?'

'No,' the Doctor said cautiously, 'I don't think it was.' He knew quite well who the woman was, but he felt that this was dangerous ground.

'He'll never tell me anything,' she said. 'But that's a girl I'd love to meet – Josephine, I mean.'

'I fancy she'd like to meet you, too,' the Doctor said politely.

'Ah, listen, Paddy,' she whispered, laying a hand on his knee, 'would you ever bring me round to her place some night? You couldn't tell Jimmy, of course. He has some daft notion that she's not class enough.'

'Not class enough? Mrs Hanrahan?'

'Ah, sure, what was my own father only a floorwalker in the Munster Arcade?' she said impatiently. 'I'd ask Kitty Lacey here to invite her, only Kitty is so blooming inquisitive. She'd want to know what you had for your dinner. And I can't help blabbing everything to her. I'm that sort, Paddy. I blab. Isn't it terrible? Do you notice the way I'm blabbing now?'

The suggestion that anyone might apply the word 'blabbing' to anything so enchanting as Roisin's conversation came to the Doctor as a shock as great as hearing himself described as an atheist and Josephine as a woman of no class. At the same time, he began to see what the dream was that gave Roisin the air of a sleepwalker. It was a dream of Jimmy. She loved the thought that he was a wild, romantic, reckless man, and when she was polishing his shoes, cooking the dinner, or bathing the child, she was sustained by that vision of him.

He was touched by it, and soon after that he took her to Josephine's little house in Rathgar. He felt nervous about doing it, but then, as I have said, the Doctor rather liked being in the position of having to be nervous. Besides, Roisin herself was in such a state that by force of comforting her he put himself at ease. She 'blabbed', as she called it, all the way.

'Tell me, Paddy, do you think I'm mad? Sometimes I think

myself I'm not in my right mind. What will Jimmy Maguire say if he hears of it? He might kill me. Did it ever strike you that he has a distinct look of Henry VIII? I call him that sometimes. He only laughs at me.'

The Doctor laughed himself at the thought of the ascetic-looking Jimmy, who resembled an El Greco saint, being compared with Henry VIII, but now that he realized Roisin had a hankering after that side of him, it struck him that if the matter were not so delicate and if only Jimmy had remained intimate with him, it might do no harm to indicate to him that an occasional touch of the firebrand would go down well at home. But Jimmy was cautiously extinguishing every bit of the firebrand in himself – either because, as Josephine thought, he was jealous, or because he wanted to get on in the world, or possibly even for a third reason, which the Doctor could not at the moment put his finger on. He had ceased to be hurt by Jimmy's defection. He was almost beginning to feel sorry for him.

The visit to Josephine was a success. When she opened the door to them, she smiled in a way that suggested that she would presently burst into tears, but as Roisin rattled on nervously, Josephine relaxed. When Roisin went upstairs for a moment, Josephine turned to the Doctor and said, 'That old humbug! He would have all the luck, wouldn't he?'

'Are you sure it's luck, dear?' the Doctor asked doubtfully.

'Why? There's nothing wrong, is there?'

'No. But I thought you said he'd regret it.'

'Oh, that!' she said with a shrug. Like all women, she lacked the courage of her intuitions.

Roisin went home after that visit and the fat was in the fire. If she had been coming back from a date with a man, she couldn't have been more terrified. For now that it was all over she realized her own duplicity. What was worse, she had made an appointment for lunch and shopping with Josephine the following week. She knelt before a picture of the Sacred Heart in her bedroom and asked for strength to be able to tell Jimmy. She explained to the Sacred Heart, as she had to the Doctor or would have explained to anyone else, that she couldn't keep a thing to herself. She was, as the Sacred Heart knew, a blabber. And she asked the Sacred Heart not to let Jimmy be too mad with her. Then, having built up a crisis out of it, she told Jimmy in an offhand way that would have made any man mad, even one without a past like Jimmy's.

'Oh, Jimmy, do you know who I ran into today? Josephine Hanrahan.' There was no response at all. 'God, Jimmy,' Roisin rattled on despairingly, 'she's a lovely woman. Why didn't you let me meet her before? We went into her place for a minute.'

'We?'

'I met her with Paddy, and she asked us in.'

Jimmy knocked the ashes out of his pipe and slowly turned on her. He frightened her. His face looked old and sour and caved in. He said, 'Does this mean you intend to defy me?'

'Defy you, Jimmy?' she said, her hands pulling nervously at her dress. 'Sure, I never defy you. I said I'd have lunch with her. Is there anything wrong with that?'

'That remains to be seen.'

'But what could I say, Jimmy? I didn't want to hurt her feelings.'

'You could have put her off,' he said. 'As you'd put off any other unsuitable invitation.'

'But I don't see what there was unsuitable about it. I liked the girl, the little I saw of her.'

'The little you saw of her, precisely,' Jimmy said, holding up his finger in warning. 'You don't really know that woman, and I do. There are things about her I'd sooner not discuss. Things I'd prefer not to say about an old friend.'

'What things, Jimmy?' Roisin asked eagerly.

'I said I'd sooner not discuss them,' Jimmy replied severely. But his training as a lawyer probably made him feel that this was unconvincing. Evidence was what was needed. 'I don't remember too well, but there was some talk about a girl in Drumcondra that jumped out of a third-storey window.'

'Is it in Drumcondra?' exclaimed Roisin, who found it difficult to keep up another person's tone. 'Sure if I was living there I'd jump out of a window myself.'

'Well, maybe it wasn't Drumcondra,' he conceded. 'Anyway, she was killed. I'm not saying it was ever brought home to Josephine. For all I know, she may be as innocent as yourself. But you do not want to be mixed up with people like that. Particularly while she's knocking around with a fellow like Paddy Baldwin.'

'Ah, for goodness' sake, you're not going to say there's anything between the pair of them!' cried Roisin. 'I don't believe a word of it, Jimmy. I think he's lonely and she just mothers him.' Jimmy laughed harshly, and she looked up at him in surprise.

'Paddy is an old friend,' he said, 'and I have no wish to criticize him. His mother, God rest her, could have told you the truth.'

'His mother?' Roisin cried incredulously. 'But Josephine says he was crazy about her.'

'She died of a broken heart,' Jimmy said.

Then he did an extraordinary thing. He went on his knees and joined his hands. You can imagine Jimmy, six foot of him, on his knees. 'Roisin,' he said, 'won't you keep away from that crowd, for my sake? You're too good for them. They'll only corrupt you the way they've corrupted others, all for their own amusement. I know them of old, and I curse the day I had anything to do with them. That's what I wanted when I married you – to get away from it all. And there's another thing,' he added, closing his eyes and staring up in agony at her like a blind man asking for a penny. 'I didn't want to tell you, but you'd better know before it's too late. My family were all a little unstable mentally. On my father's side, of course. I couldn't bear a mental shock. My uncle was insane when he died. You wouldn't want to drive me to that.'

'Your uncle?' Roisin cried. 'Which uncle?'

'Willie,' he replied humbly. 'It was kept a great secret. We didn't want anyone to know.'

'I think,' Roisin said, speaking with real indignation, 'I might have been told before now.'

Extraordinary as it was for her to see this great man at her feet, it wasn't him she was thinking of now. It was Little Liam. Liam was a curious child. He always hated to be denied anything, and if you spoke severely to him he screamed with rage. Was it possible that Liam had inherited the family weakness, and had she in her innocence made it worse by frustrating him when she should have comforted him and given in to him? For the first time she was really angry with Jimmy, and went upstairs to look at the child, and then knelt by his bedside and promised the Sacred Heart that she would never cross him again, whatever he wanted.

She was a serious girl, and she knew that she could not imperil her marriage by doing something that Jimmy disapproved of, so she rang up Josephine and excused herself because of illness. But she was also a rotten liar. When Josephine, a woman who'd give you the shift off her back, heard that Roisin was ill, she announced that she was coming over to look after the house for her. Then Roisin's heart misgave her, and she asked Josephine over for tea. She felt terrible about it because she knew that she was no good at explaining things if the explanation involved any improbabilities, and she was certain that Josephine would see through it all. She did. Within five minutes she knew that Roisin was acting under Jimmy's orders and went white with rage. It was bad enough that he would not invite her to the house. To make it plain that he did not think her a proper acquaintance for his wife was too much. When he was ill and a bachelor, he simply packed his bag and came to her house and stayed there till he was well. So she told

Roisin this, and Roisin shook her head despairingly.

'What can I do?' she asked.

'Whatever you like,' said Josephine. 'I wouldn't allow my husband to give me orders like that.'

Roisin realized unhappily that a partial explanation was not enough. 'But it isn't only that, Josephine,' she said. 'I'm afraid to contradict him. You see, it's in the family. He had an uncle that was queer.'

'It's the first I've heard of it,' Josephine said.

'Well, to tell you the truth, it's the first I heard of it, too,' said Roisin.

'But who told you?' Josephine persisted.

'He did – Jimmy, I mean. He told me it was dangerous for him to be upset.'

'And you're quite sure he's not making it up?'

'Would a man say a thing like that about his own family if it wasn't true? Sure, that would be crazy out and out. I'd sooner 'twas true. You don't think it isn't?' she added anxiously.

'I'll make it my business to find out,' Josephine said grimly.

'But if that's not true,' Roisin wailed, 'then I suppose Paddy's mother didn't die of a broken heart, either.'

'Paddy's mother?' cried Josephine. 'She worshipped the ground he walked on. And with good reason. I don't know what's come over your husband, Roisin. I never knew him to tell lies like that.'

'It isn't lying, that's the awful part of it,' Roisin said in distress. 'Josephine, I've never breathed it to a soul, and I wouldn't say it now only I know it's not true. Actually, I knew all the time it wasn't true. You will understand me, won't you? I'm only telling you to show how crazy he is. That woman in Drumcondra that was supposed to have committed suicide because of you . . .'

At that point, Josephine nearly went crazy herself, and nothing but loyalty to Roisin prevented her from going straight to Jimmy's office and demanding a signed retraction. Anyway, it made no difference. For if there is one impression a man must never leave upon his wife it is that he is emotional and unstable, because it means that the woman at once begins to feel the whole business of judgement and decision devolves upon her, and a woman who feels that no longer respects her husband. So Roisin continued to meet the gang, and take one drink, which always made her tight, and she developed a violent crush on Con Bishop, whose Oxford accent probably reminded her of Henry VIII. She and Josephine were devoted to one another, though not in the way Roisin would have wished, with Josephine as the confidante of her passion for Jimmy. Rather, she was the confidante of Roisin's doubts of Jimmy, the woman she would rush to whenever there was trouble between them. Jimmy, on the other hand, for ever alienated from all his old friends by his slanders, took to going to chapel in the evenings and praying that his wife would not do something it would have taken a convulsion of nature to make her do, and at home he was ordered about as if he were a child.

(1966)

THE AMERICAN WIFE

ELSIE COLLEARY, who was on a visit to her cousins in Cork, was a mystery even to them. Her father, Jack Colleary's brother, had emigrated when he was a kid and done well for himself; he had made his money in the liquor business, and left it to go into wholesale produce when Elsie was growing up, because he didn't think it was the right background for a girl. He had given her the best of educations, and all he had got out of it was to have Elsie telling him that Irishmen were more manly, and that even Irish-Americans let their wives boss them too much. What she meant was that *he* let her mother boss him, and she had learned from other Irish people that this was not the custom at home. Maybe Mike Colleary, like a lot of other Americans, did give the impression of yielding too much to his wife, but that was because she thought she knew more about things than he did, and he was too softhearted to disillusion her. No doubt the Americans, experienced in nostalgia, took Elsie's glorification of Irishmen good-humouredly, but it did not go down too well in Cork, where the men stood in perpetual contemplation of the dangers of marriage, like cranes standing on one leg at the edge of the windy water.

She stood out at the Collearys' quiet little parties, with her high waist and wide skirts, taking the men out to sit on the stairs while she argued with them about religion and politics. Women having occasion to go upstairs thought this very forward, but some of the men found it a pleasant relief. Besides, like all Americans, she was probably a millionaire, and the most unworldly of men can get a kick out of flirting with a real millionaire.

The man she finally fell in love with did not sit on the stairs with her at all, though, like her, he was interested in religion and politics. This was a chap called Tom Barry. Tom was thirty-five, tall and thin and good-looking, and he lived with his mother and two good-looking sisters in a tiny house near the barrack, and he couldn't even go for a walk in the evening without the three of them lining up in the hallway to present him with his hat, his gloves, and his clean handkerchief. He had a small job in the courthouse, and was not without ambition; he had engaged in several small business enterprises with his friend Jerry Coakley, but all they had ever got out of these was some good stories. Jerry was forty, and *he* had an old mother who insisted on putting his socks on for him.

Elsie's cousins warned her against setting her cap at Tom, but this only seemed to make her worse. 'I guess I'll have to seduce him,' she replied airily, and her cousins, who had never known a well-bred Catholic girl to talk like that, were shocked. She shocked them even more before she was done. She called at his house when she knew he wasn't there and deluded his innocent mother and sisters into believing that she didn't have designs on him; she badgered Tom to death at the office, gave him presents, and even hired a car to take him for drives.

They weren't the only ones who were shocked. Tom was shocked himself when she asked him point-blank how much he earned. However, he put that down to unworldliness and told her.

'But that's not even a street-cleaner's wages at home,' she said indignantly.

'I'm sure, Elsie,' he said sadly. 'But then, of course, money isn't everything.'

'No, and Ireland isn't everything,' she replied. It was peculiar, but from their first evening together she had never ceased talking about America to him – the summer heat, and the crickets chattering, and the leaves alive with fireflies. During her discussions on the stairs, she had apparently discovered a great many things wrong with Ireland, and Tom, with a sort of mournful pleasure, kept adding to them.

'Oh, I know, I know,' he said regretfully.

'Then if you know, why don't you do something about it?'

'Ah, well, I suppose it's habit, Elsie,' he said as though he wasn't quite sure. 'I suppose I'm too old to learn new tricks.'

But Elsie doubted if it was really habit, and it perplexed her that a man so clever and conscientious could at the same time be so lacking in initiative. She explained it finally to herself in terms of an attachment to his mother that was neither natural nor healthy. Elsie was a girl who loved explanations.

On their third outing she had proposed to him, and he was so astonished that he burst out laughing, and continued to laugh whenever he thought of it again. Elsie herself couldn't see anything to laugh at in it. Having been proposed to by men who were younger and better-looking and better-off than he was, she felt she had been conferring an honour on him. But he was a curious man, for when she repeated the proposal, he said, with a cold fury that hurt her, 'Sometimes I wish you'd think before you talk, Elsie. You know what I earn, and you know it isn't enough to keep a family on. Besides, in case you haven't noticed, I have a mother and two sisters to support.'

'You could earn enough to support them in America,' she protested.

'And I told you already that I had no intention of going to America.'

'I have some money of my own,' she said. 'It's not much, but it could mean I'd be no burden to you.'

'Listen, Elsie,' he said, 'a man who can't support a wife and children has no business marrying at all. I have no business marrying anyway. I'm not a very cheerful man, and I have a rotten temper.'

Elsie went home in tears, and told her astonished uncle that all Irishmen were pansies, and, as he had no notion what pansies were, he shook his head and admitted that it was a terrible country. Then she wrote to Tom and told him that what he needed was not a wife but a psychiatrist. The writing of this gave her great satisfaction, but next morning she realized that her mother would only say she had been silly. Her mother believed that men needed careful handling. The day after, she waited for Tom outside the courthouse, and when he came out she summoned him with two angry blasts on the horn. A rainy sunset was flooding the Western Road with yellow light that made her look old and grim.

'Well,' she said bitterly, 'I'd hoped I'd never see your miserable face again.'

But that extraordinary man only smiled gently and rested his elbows on the window of the car.

'I'm delighted you came,' he said. 'I was all last night trying to write to you, but I'm not very good at it.'

'Oh, so you got my letter?'

'I did, and I'm ashamed to have upset you so much. All I wanted to say was that if you're serious – I mean really serious – about this, I'd be honoured.'

At first she thought he was mocking her. Then she realized that he wasn't, and she was in such an evil humour that she was tempted to tell him she had changed her mind. Then common-sense told her the man would be fool enough to believe her, and after that his pride wouldn't let him propose to her again. It was the price you had to pay for dealing with men who had such a high notion of their own dignity.

'I suppose it depends on whether you love me or not,' she replied. 'It's a little matter you forgot to mention.'

He raised himself from the car window, and in the evening light she saw a look of positive pain on his lean, sad, gentle face. 'Ah, I do, but—' he was beginning when she cut him off and told him to get in the car. Whatever he was about to say, she didn't want to hear it.

They settled down in a modern bungalow outside the town, on the edge of the harbour. Elsie's mother, who flew over for the wedding, said dryly that she hoped Elsie would be able to make up to Tom for the loss of his mother's services. In fact, it wasn't long before the Barrys were saying she wasn't, and making remarks about her cooking and her lack of tidiness. But if Tom noticed there was anything wrong, which is improbable, he didn't mention it. Whatever his faults as a sweetheart, he made a good husband. It may have been the affection of a sensitive man for someone he saw as frightened, fluttering, and insecure. It could have been the longing of a frustrated one for someone that seemed to him remote, romantic, and mysterious. But whatever it was, Tom, who had always been God Almighty to his mother and sisters, was extraordinarily patient and understanding with Elsie, and she needed it, because she was often homesick and scared.

Jerry Coakley was a great comfort to her in these fits, for Jerry had a warmth of manner that Tom lacked. He was an insignificant-looking man with a ravaged dyspeptic face and a tubercular complexion, a thin, bitter mouth with bad teeth, and long, lank hair; but he was so sympathetic and insinuating that at times he even gave you the impression that he was changing his shape to suit your mood. Elsie had the feeling that the sense of failure had eaten deeper into him than into Tom.

At once she started to arrange a match between him and Tom's elder sister, Annie, in spite of Tom's warnings that Jerry would never marry till his mother died. When she realized that Tom was right, she said it was probably as well, because Annie wouldn't put his socks on him. Later she admitted that this was unfair, and that it would probably be a great relief to poor Jerry to be allowed to put on his socks himself. Between Tom and him there was one of those passionate relationships that spring up in small towns where society narrows itself down to a handful of erratic and explosive friendships. There were always people who weren't talking to other people, and friends had all to be dragged into the disagreement, no matter how trifling it might be, and often it happened that the principals had already become fast friends again when *their* friends were still ignoring one another in the street. But Jerry and Tom refused to disagree. Jerry would drop in for a bottle of stout, and Tom and he would denounce the country, while Elsie wondered why they could never find anything more interesting to talk about than stupid priests and crooked politicians.

Elsie's causes were of a different kind. The charwoman, Mrs Dorgan, had six children and a husband who didn't earn enough to keep them. Elsie concealed from Tom how much she really paid Mrs Dorgan, but she couldn't conceal that Mrs Dorgan wore her clothes, or that she took the Dorgan family to the seaside in the summer. When Jerry suggested to Tom that the Dorgans might be doing too well out of Elsie, Tom replied, 'Even if they were, Jerry, I wouldn't interfere. If 'tis people's nature to be generous, you must let them be generous.'

For Tom's causes she had less patience. 'Oh, why don't you people do something about it, instead of talking?' she cried.

'What could you do, Elsie?' asked Jerry.

'At least you could show them up,' said Elsie.

'Why, Elsie?' he asked with his mournful smile. 'Were you thinking of starting a paper?'

'Then, if you can't do anything about it, shut up!' she said. 'You and Tom seem to get some queer masochistic pleasure out of these people.'

'Begor, Elsie, you might have something there,' Jerry said, nodding ruefully.

'Oh, we adore them,' Tom said mockingly.

'You do,' she said. 'I've seen you. You sit here night after night denouncing them, and then when one of them gets sick you're round to the house to see if there's anything you can do for him, and when he dies you start a collection for his wife and family. You make me sick.' Then she stamped out to the kitchen.

Jerry hunched his shoulders and exploded in splutters and giggles. He reached out a big paw for a bottle of stout, with the air of someone snaring a rabbit.

'I declare to God, Tom, she has us taped,' he said.

'She has you taped anyway,' said Tom.

'How's that?'

'She thinks you need an American wife as well.'

'Well, now, she mightn't be too far out in that, either,' said Jerry with a crooked grin. 'I often thought it would take something like that.'

'She thinks you have *problems*,' said Tom with a snort. Elsie's favourite word gave him the creeps.

'She wouldn't be referring to the mother, by any chance?'

For a whole year Elsie had fits of depression because she thought she wasn't going to have a baby, and she saw several doctors, whose advice she repeated in mixed company, to the great embarrassment of everybody except Jerry. After that, for the best part of another year, she had fits of depression because she was going to have a baby, and she informed everybody about that as well, including the occasion of its conception and the probable date of its arrival, and again they were all embarrassed except Jerry. Having reached the age of eighteen before learning that there was any real difference between the sexes, Jerry found all her talk fascinating, and also he realized that Elsie saw nothing immodest in it. It was just that she had an experimental interest in her body and mind. When she gave him Bourbon he studied its taste, but when he gave her Irish she studied its effect–it was as simple as that. Jerry, too, liked explanations, but he liked them for their own sake, and not with the intention of doing anything with them. At the same time, Elsie was scared by what she thought was a lack of curiosity on the part of the Cork doctors, and when her mother learned this she began to press Elsie to have the baby in America, where she would feel secure.

'You don't think I should go back, Tom?' she asked guilt-ily. 'Daddy says he'll pay my fare.'

It came as a shock to Tom, though the idea had crossed his mind that something of the kind might happen. 'If that's the way you feel about it, I suppose you'd better, Elsie,' he re-plied.

'But you wouldn't come with me.'

'How can I come with you? You know I can't just walk out of the office for a couple of months.'

'But you could get a job at home.'

'And I told you a dozen times I don't want a job in Am-erica,' he said angrily. Then, seeing the way it upset her, he changed his tone. 'Look, if you stay here, feeling the way you do, you'll work yourself into a real illness. Anyway, some time you'll have to go back on a visit, and this is as good an occasion as any.'

'But how can I, without you?' she asked. 'You'd only neglect yourself.'

'I would not neglect myself.'

'Would you stay at your mother's?'

'I would not stay at my mother's. This is my house, and I'm going to stop here.'

Tom worried less about the effect Elsie's leaving would have on him than about what his family would say, par-ticularly Annie, who never lost the chance of a crack at Elsie. 'You let that girl walk on you, Tom Barry,' she said. 'One of these days she'll walk too hard.' Then, of course, Tom walked on *her*, in the way that only a devoted brother can, but that was no relief to the feeling that something had come between Elsie and him and that he could do nothing about it. When he was driving Elsie to the liner, he knew that she felt the same, for she didn't break down until they came to a long grey bridge over an inlet of water, guarded by a lonely grey stone tower. She had once pointed it out to him as the first thing she had seen that represented Ireland to her, and now he had the feeling that this was how she saw him – a battered old tower by a river mouth that was no longer of any importance to anyone but the seagulls.

She was away longer than she or anyone else had expected. First there was the wedding of an old schoolfriend; then her mother's birthday; then the baby got ill. It was clear that she was enjoying herself immensely, but she wrote long and frequent letters, sent snapshots of herself and the baby, and – most important of all – had named the baby for Jerry Coakley. Clearly Elsie hadn't forgotten them. The Dorgan kids appeared on the road in clothes that had obviously been made in America, and whenever Tom met them he stopped to speak to them and give them the pennies he thought Elsie would have given them.

Occasionally Tom went to his mother's for supper, but otherwise he looked after himself. Nothing could persuade him that he was not a natural housekeeper, or that whatever his sisters could do he could not do just as well himself. Sometimes Jerry came and the two men took off their coats and tried to prepare a meal out of one of Elsie's cookbooks. 'Steady, squad!' Tom would murmur as he wiped his hands before taking another peep at the book. 'You never know when this might come in handy.' But whether it was the result of Tom's supervision or Jerry's helplessness, the meal usually ended in a big burn-up, or a tasteless mess from which some essential ingredient seemed to be missing, and they laughed over it as they consoled themselves with bread and cheese and stout. 'Elsie is right,' Jerry would say, shaking his head regretfully. 'We have problems, boy! We have problems!'

Elsie returned at last with trunks full of new clothes, a box of up-to-date kitchen stuff, and a new gaiety and energy. Every ten minutes Tom would make an excuse to tiptoe upstairs and take another look at his son. Then the Barrys arrived, and Elsie gave immediate offence by quoting Gesell and Spock. But Mrs Barry didn't seem to mind as much as her daughters. By some extraordinary process of association, she had discovered a great similarity between Elsie and herself in the fact that she had married from the south side of the city into the north and had never got used to it. This delighted Elsie, who went about proclaiming that her mother-in-law and herself were both displaced persons.

The next year was a very happy one, and less trying on Elsie, because she had another woman to talk to, even if most of the time she didn't understand what her mother-in-law was telling her, and had the suspicion that her mother-in-law didn't understand her either. But then she got pregnant for the second time, and became restless and dissatisfied once more, though now it wasn't only with hospitals and doctors but with schools and schoolteachers as well. Tom and Jerry had impressed on her that the children were being turned into idiots, learning through the medium of a language they didn't understand – indeed, according to Tom, it was a language that nobody understood. What chance would the children have?

'Ah, I suppose the same chance as the rest of us, Elsie,' said Jerry in his sly, mournful way.

'But you and Tom don't want chances, Jerry,' she replied earnestly. 'Neither of you has any ambition.'

'Ah, you should look on the bright side of things. Maybe with God's help they won't have any ambition either.'

But this time it had gone beyond a joke. For days on end Tom was in a rage with her, and when he was angry he seemed to withdraw into himself like a snail into a shell.

Unable to get at him, Elsie grew hysterical. 'It's all your damned obstinacy,' she sobbed. 'You don't do anything in this rotten hole, but you're too conceited to get out of it. Your family treat you as if you were God, and then you behave to me as if you were. God! God! God!' she screamed, and each time she punched him viciously with her fist, till suddenly the humour of their situations struck him and he went off into laughter.

After that he could only make his peace with her and make excuses for her leaving him again, but he knew that the excuses wouldn't impress his sisters. One evening when he went to see them, Annie caught him, as she usually did, when he was going out the front door, and he stood looking sidewise down the avenue.

'Are you letting Elsie go off to America again, Tom?' she asked.

'I don't know,' Tom said, pulling his long nose with an air of affected indifference. 'I can't very well stop her, can I?'

'Damn soon she'd be stopped if she hadn't the money,' said Annie. 'And you're going to let her take young Jerry?'

'Ah, how could I look after Jerry? Talk sense, can't you!'

'And I suppose we couldn't look after him either? We're not sufficiently well read.'

'Ah, the child should be with his own mother, Annie,' Tom said impatiently.

'And where should his mother be? Ah, Tom Barry,' she added bitterly, 'I told you what that one was, and she's not done with you yet. Are you sure she's going to bring him back?'

Then Tom exploded on her in his cold, savage way. 'If you want to know, I am not,' he said, and strode down the avenue with his head slightly bowed.

Something about the cut of him as he passed under a street lamp almost broke Annie's heart. 'The curse of God on that bitch!' she said when she returned to her mother in the kitchen.

'Is it Elsie?' her mother cried angrily. 'How dare you talk of her like that!'

'He's letting her go to America again,' said Annie.

'He's a good boy, and he's right to consider her feelings,' said her mother anxiously. 'I often thought myself I'd go back to the south side and not be ending my days in this misfortunate hole.'

The months after Elsie's second departure were bitter ones for Tom. A house from which a woman is gone is bad enough, but one from which a child is gone is a dead house.

Tom would wake in the middle of the night thinking he heard Jerry crying, and be half out of bed before he realized that Jerry was thousands of miles away. He did not continue his experiments with cooking and housekeeping. He ate at his mother's, spent most of his time at the Coakleys, and drank far too much. Like all inward-looking men he had a heavy hand on the bottle. Meanwhile Elsie wavered and procrastinated worse than before, setting dates, cancelling her passage, sometimes changing her mind within twenty-four hours. In his despondency Tom resigned himself to the idea that she wouldn't return at all, or at least persuaded himself that he had.

'Oh, she'll come back all right,' Jerry said with a worried air. 'The question is, will she stay back . . . You don't mind me talking about it?' he asked.

'Indeed no. Why would I?'

'You know, Tom, I'd say ye had family enough to last ye another few years.'

Tom didn't look up for a few moments, and when he did he smiled faintly. 'You think it's that?'

'I'm not saying she knows it,' Jerry added hastily. 'There's nothing calculating about her, and she's crazy about you.'

'I thought it was something that went with having the baby,' Tom said thoughtfully. 'Some sort of homing instinct.'

'I wouldn't say so,' said Jerry. 'Not altogether. I think she feels that eventually she'll get you through the kids.'

'She won't,' Tom said bitterly.

'I know, sure, I know. But Elsie can't get used to the – the irremediable.' The last word was so unlike Jerry that Tom felt he must have looked it up in a dictionary, and the absurdity of this made him feel very close to his old crony. 'Tell me, Tom,' Jerry added gently, 'wouldn't you do it? I know it wouldn't be easy, but wouldn't you try it, even for a while, for Elsie's sake? 'Twould mean a hell of a lot to her.'

'I'm too old, Jerry,' Tom said so deliberately that Jerry knew it had been in his mind as well.

'Oh, I know, I know,' Jerry repeated. 'Even ten years ago I might have done it myself. It's like jail. The time comes when you're happier in than out. And that's not the worst of it,' he added bitterly. 'The worst is when you pretend you like it.'

It was a strange evening that neither of them ever forgot, sitting in that little house to which Elsie's absence seemed a rebuke, and listening to the wind from the harbour that touched the foot of the garden. They knew they belonged to a country whose youth was always escaping from it, out beyond that harbour, and that was middle-aged in all its attitudes and institutions. Of those that remained, a little handful lived with defeat and learned fortitude and humour and sweetness, and these were the things that Elsie, with her generous idealism, loved in them. But she couldn't pay the price. She wanted them where she belonged herself, among the victors.

A few weeks later Elsie was back; the house was full of life again, and that evening seemed only a bad dream. It was almost impossible to keep Jerry Og, as they called the elder child, away from Tom. He was still only a baby, and a spoiled one at that, but when Tom took him to the village Jerry Og thrust out his chest and took strides that were too big for him, like any small boy with a father he adored. Each day, he lay in wait for the postman and then took the post away to sort it for himself. He sorted it by the pictures on the stamps, and Elsie noted gleefully that he reserved all the pretty pictures for his father.

Nobody had remembered Jerry's good advice, even Jerry himself, and eighteen months later Elsie was pregnant again. Again their lives took the same pattern of unrest. But this time Elsie was even more distressed than Tom.

'I'm a curse to you,' she said. 'There's something wrong with me. I can't be natural.'

'Oh, you're natural enough,' Tom replied bitterly. 'You married the wrong man, that's all.'

'I didn't, I didn't!' she protested despairingly. 'You can say anything else but that. If I believed that, I'd have nothing left, because I never cared for anyone but you. And in spite of what you think, I'm coming back,' she went on, in tears. 'I'm coming back if it kills me. God, I hate this country; I hate every goddamn thing about it; I hate what it's done to you and Jerry. But I'm not going to let you go.'

'You have no choice,' Tom said patiently. 'Jerry Og will have to go to school, and you can't be bringing him hither and over, even if you could afford it.'

'Then, if that's what you feel, why don't you keep him?' she cried. 'You know perfectly well you could stop me taking him with me if you wanted to. You wouldn't even have to bring me into court. I'll give him to you now. Isn't that proof enough that I'm coming back?'

'No, Elsie, it is not,' Tom replied, measuring every word. 'And I'm not going to bring you into court, either. I'm not going to take hostages to make sure my wife comes back to me.'

And though Elsie continued to delude herself with the belief that she would return, she knew Tom was right. It would all appear different when she got home. The first return to Ireland had been hard, the second had seemed impossible. Yet, even in the black hours when she really considered the situation, she felt she could never resign herself to something that had been determined before she was born, and she deceived herself with the hope that Tom would change his mind and follow her. He must follow her. Even if he was prepared to abandon her he would never abandon Jerry Og.

And this, as Big Jerry could have told her, was where she made her biggest mistake, because if Tom had done it at all it would have been for her. But Big Jerry had decided that the whole thing had gone beyond his power to help. He recognized the irremediable, all right, sometimes perhaps even before it became irremediable. But that, as he would have said himself, is where the ferryboat had left him.

Thanks to Elsie, the eldest of the Dorgans now has a job in

Boston and in the course of years the rest of them will probably go there as well. Tom continues to live in his little bungalow beside the harbour. Annie is keeping house for him, which suits her fine, because Big Jerry's old mother continued to put his socks on for him a few years too long, and now Annie has only her brother to worship. To all appearances they are happy enough, as happiness goes in Cork. Jerry still calls, and the two men discuss the terrible state of the country. But in Tom's bedroom there are pictures of Elsie and the children, the third of whom he knows only through photographs, and, apart from that, nothing has changed since Elsie left it five years ago. It is a strange room, for one glance is enough to show that the man who sleeps there is still in love, and that everything that matters to him in the world is reflected there. And one day, if he comes by the dollars, he will probably go out and visit them all, but it is here he will return and here, no doubt, he will die.

(1961)

THE CHEAT

I

THE only thing that distinguished Dick Gordon from the other young men of my time in Cork was his attitude to religion. As an engineer he seemed to feel that he could not afford to believe in anything but the second law of thermodynamics: according to him, this contained everything a man required to know.

For years he courted a girl called Joan Twomey, and everyone expected he would marry her and settle down, as most men of his kind do. Usually they are of a serious disposition and settle down more easily than the rest of humanity. You often see them in their later years, carrying round the collection bag at twelve-o'clock Mass, and wonder what has happened to all their wild dreams of free thought and social justice. Marriage is the great leveller.

But Joan's mother died, and she had to do the housekeeping for a father and two younger sisters, so she became serious too, and there was no more reckless behaviour in the little seaside house they rented in summer. She was afraid of marrying a man who did not believe in anything and would probably bring up his children the same way. She was wrong in this, because Dick was much too tolerant a man to deprive his worst enemy of the pleasure of believing in eternal damnation, much less his wife, but Joan's seriousness had developed to the dimensions of spiritual pride and she gave him up as she might have given up some pleasure for Lent.

Dick was mystified and hurt: it was the first shock to his feeling of the basic reasonableness of life; but he did n̶ allow it to change him. After all, his brother, To an ex-cleric, and he had been worked on by experts. Some time later he met a girl called Barbara Hough, who was a teacher in a Protestant school, and started to walk out with her. On the surface Barbara was much more his style. She was good-looking and urbane, vaguely atheistic and left-wing in her views, and she thought that all Irish people, Catholic and Protestant, were quite insane on the subject of religion. All the same, for a young fellow of good Catholic family to take up with a Protestant at all was a challenge, and Barbara, who was a high-spirited girl, enjoyed it and made the most of it. His friends were amused and his family alarmed. Of course, Dick could get a dispensation if Barbara signed the paper guaranteeing that their children would be brought up as Catholics, but would Barbara, who was a rector's daughter, agree to it? Characteristically, when Tom asked him this, Dick only smiled and said, 'Funny, isn't it? I never asked her.' He would probably have been quite safe in doing so, for though Barbara herself did not recognize it, she had all the loneliness of one brought up in a minority religion, always feeling that she was missing something, and much of Dick's appeal for her was that he was a Prince Charming who had broken the magic circle in which she felt she would be trapped until the day she died. But Dick did not ask her. Instead he proposed a quiet registry-office marriage in London, and she was so moved by his consideration for her that she did not even anticipate what the consequences might be.

You see, it was part of Dick's simplicity of mind that he could not realize that there were certain perfectly simple things you couldn't do without involving yourself in more trouble than they were worth, or, if he did see it, he underrated its importance. A few of his old friends stood by him, but even they had to admit that there was an impossible streak in him. When Barbara was having a baby the family deputed his brother, Tom, to warn him of what he was doing. Tom was tall, good-looking, dreamy and morbidly sensitive. He did not want to approach Dick at all, but seeing that he was the nearest thing to a priest in the family, he felt that it might be his duty.

'You know what people are going to think, Dick,' he said with a stammer.

'The same as they think now, I suppose,' Dick replied with his gentle smile.

'This is different, Dick.'

'How, Tom?'

'This concerns a third party, you see,' said Tom, too embarrassed even to mention such things as babies to his brother.

'And a fourth and a fifth, I hope,' Dick said cheerfully. 'It's a natural result of marriage, you know. And children do take after their parents, for the first few years anyway.'

'Not in this country, they don't,' Tom said ruefully. 'I suppose there are historical reasons for it,' he added, being a great student of history.

'There are historical reasons for everything in this country, Tom,' said Dick with a jolly laugh. 'But because some old fool believes in the fairies for good historical reasons is no excuse for bringing up my kids the same way.'

'Ah, well, it's not as foolish as all that, Dick,' said Tom, looking more miserable than ever. 'It's poetic, or fanciful or whatever you like, but it's what we were brought up to believe, and our fathers and grandfathers before us.'

'And the monks told us that Ireland was such a holy country that we'd have the end of the world eight years before anywhere else ... I'm not sure what the advantage was supposed to be ... I don't suppose you still believe that?'

'Why would I?' asked Tom. 'It's not an article of faith.'

'It was an article of faith to you and me, and I wouldn't have liked to be the fellow that disbelieved it,' said Dick with a sniff. 'Anyway, it's no worse than the rest of the nonsense we listen to. That sort of thing is looked on as childishness everywhere else today, and it'll be looked on as childishness here, too, in your lifetime and mine. In fifteen years' time people will only laugh at it.'

That was Dick all out, entirely reasonable and tolerant, and yet as big a misfit as if he had two heads. How could any responsible superior recommend a man as pig-headed as that for promotion? The sensible thing for Dick would have been to emigrate and start all over again in England or America, where apparitions were not so highly regarded, but there was a dogged, cynical streak in him that derived a sort of morose pleasure from seeing some devotee of apparitions promoted over his head and making a mess of some perfectly simple job.

He had a number of friends who sympathized with his views and who met at his little house in the College Road on Sundays to discuss the latest piece of jobbery in the university. They grew mad about it, but Dick's attitude of amused tolerance rarely varied. At most he sighed: it was as though he saw things that they could not see. One old schoolteacher called Murphy used to grow furious with him over this. He was a gloomy-looking, handsome man who was at the same time very pious and very anti-clerical. Passion made him break out in angles, as when he called his old friends 'Mister'.

'Mister Gordon,' he shouted one night, 'you're out of your mind. A hundred years from now the descendants of those hobblers will still be seeing apparitions behind every bush.'

'They won't, Ned,' Dick said with a smile. He was particularly fond of Murphy and enjoyed seeing him in a rage.

'What'll stop them, Mister Gordon?'

'Facts, Ned!'

'Facts!'

'Facts impose their own logic, Ned. They're imposing it now, at this very minute, here and elsewhere, even though we may not see it. It's only an elaboration of skills. Skills here are still too rudimentary. But women are beginning to do men's work, and they'll have to think men's thoughts. You can't control that, you know. The world you're talking about is finished. In ten or fifteen years' time it'll be a joke. Simple facts will destroy it.'

2

That was all very well. Dick might have a good eye for what was going on in the outside world, but he had no eye at all for what was going on in his very own house. One evening, after they had been married for ten years, Dick was at home and Barbara out with their son, Tom, when there was a knock at the door. Outside was a young priest; a tall, thin, good-looking man with a devil-may-care eye.

'Can I come in?' he asked, as though he had no doubt whatever of his welcome.

'Oh, come in, come in!' said Dick with a thin smile. He hated those embarrassing occasions when people with more self-confidence than manners inquired how his soul was doing. He was a friendly man and did not like to have to appear rude or ungrateful.

'Mrs G out?' the priest asked cheerfully.

'Yes, gone into town for some messages,' Dick said resignedly. 'She won't be long.'

'Ah, it gives us the chance of a little chat,' said the priest, pulling at the legs of his trousers.

'Look, Father, I don't want a little chat, as you call it,' Dick said appealingly. 'This town is full of people who want little chats with me, and they can't understand that I don't appreciate them. I gave up religion when I was eighteen, and I have no intention in the world of going back to it.'

'Did I ask you to go back to it?' the priest asked with an air of consternation. 'I wasn't expecting to see you at all, man! I came here to talk to your wife. You are Mrs Gordon's husband, aren't you?'

'Yes,' Dick replied, somewhat surprised by the priest's tone.

'Well, she's been receiving instruction. Didn't you know that?'

'Instruction? No, I didn't.'

'Crumbs, I'm after saying the wrong thing again!' the priest said angrily. 'I shouldn't be let out without a male nurse. Look, I'm terribly sorry. I'll come back another time.'

'Oh, as you're here, you may as well stay,' Dick said amiably. It was partly pride, partly pity. He could see that the priest was genuinely distressed.

'Another time! Another time!'

'Who will I say called?' Dick asked as he saw him to the door.

'The name is Hogan. Mr Gordon, I wouldn't have wished it for a hundred pounds.'

'It was hardly your fault,' Dick said, with a friendly smile.

But as he closed the door the smile faded and he found himself cold and shaking. He poured himself a drink, but it only made him feel sick. Nothing that could have happened to him would have been quite so bad as this. He had been betrayed shamelessly and treacherously, and he could already see himself as the laughing-stock of the city. A man's loneliness is his strength and only a wife can really destroy him because only she can understand his loneliness.

He heard her key in the lock and wished he had left before her return. He liked to be master of himself, and now he feared he had no control over what he did or said.

'Dick!' she called in her clear ringing voice and opened the living-room door. 'Is something wrong?' she asked as he did not turn round. 'One moment, Tom!' she said to the child in the hall. 'Run upstairs and take your things off. I'll call you when tea is ready. Don't argue now, sweetheart. Mummy is busy.' She closed the door behind her and approached him. 'I suppose Father Hogan called,' she added in her weary, well-bred voice. 'Was that it? You should know I intended to tell you. I wanted to make up my own mind first.' Still he did not reply and she burst out into a wail, 'Oh, Dick, I've tried to tell you so often and I didn't have the courage.'

She knew the moment he looked at her that she had fooled herself; persuaded herself that he was dull and tolerant and gentle and that nothing she did to him would affect their relationship. It is the weak spot in the cheat, man or woman.

'You hadn't the courage,' he repeated dully. 'But you had the courage to make a fool of me before your clerical friends.'

'I didn't, Dick,' she said hotly. 'But you know yourself it's something I can't discuss with you. It's a subject you can't be reasonable about.'

The word 'reasonable' stung him.

'Is that what you call being reasonable?' he asked bitterly. 'I should have been reasonable and made you conform before I married you. I should have been reasonable and brought Tom up as my family wanted him brought up. Every day of my life I had to accept humiliation on your account when I could have been reasonable about it all. And then you don't even have the courage to discuss with me what you're going to do or what the consequences will be for Tom. You prefer to bring him up believing that his father is damned! There's reasonableness for you!'

'But I'd discuss it with you now, Dick, if only you'd listen to me patiently.' She began to wring her hands. 'It's not my fault if I can't live without believing in something.'

'In Heaven,' he said cynically.

'In Heaven, if you like. Anyway, in something for you and me and Tom. I was brought up to believe in it, and I threw it away because I didn't value it, and now I need it — maybe because I haven't anything else. If only you wouldn't tell me it's all just nonsense!'

'Why should I tell you anything?' he asked. 'You have better advisers now.'

In fact, he never did discuss it with her. He even allowed

Tom to go to Mass with her and attend the local monks'
school without protest. The older Tom was Barbara's biggest
surprise. She knew that in arguments with Dick he had
taken her side, but when they discussed it together he
seemed to judge her far more severely than Dick. It was
curious, because the diffidence, the slight stammer, the
charming smile did not change.

'Of course, Barbara, as a Catholic I am naturally pleased,
for your sake and the kid's, but as Dick's brother I can't help
feeling that it's unfortunate.'

'But don't you think it may help Dick to see things a bit
differently in the course of time?'

'No, Barbara, I don't,' he said with a gentle, almost pitying
smile.

'But, Tom, I don't see that it should make any more
difference than it does between you and Dick.'

'Marriage is different, Barbara,' he said, and she didn't
even see anything peculiar about being told of marriage by a
man who had almost been given up by his own family as
unmarriageable. 'People don't know it, but they marry for
protection as much as anything else, and sometimes they
have to be protected at the cost of other people's prin-
ciples.'

'And you think Dick needs protection?' she asked wonderingly.

'I think Dick needs a great deal of protection, Barbara,' he
said with an accusing look.

There was a good deal of talk in the city, much of it ill-
natured, though on the whole it did Dick less harm than
good. He had ceased to be an active force for evil and
become a mere figure of fun, as vulnerable to ridicule as any
university intriguer. It had even become safe to promote
him.

But it was old Ned Murphy who said the thing that stuck.
He and two of Dick's other friends were drinking in a
public-house one night, and the others – Cashman, and Enright who was a bit of a smart alec – were making good-

humoured fun of Dick. Murphy alone did not laugh at all. He scowled and rubbed his forehead with his fist till it grew inflamed.

'It's like your wife having an affair with another man,' he said sourly, and because he was unmarried Cashman and Enright laughed louder. Still there was something uncomfortably apt about the analogy; both were married men and there had been a small scandal about Enright's wife, who had had an affair with a commercial traveller. They knew there was always another man, a shadowy figure, not real as they were, and they dreaded his presence in the background.

'Still, you'd think he'd have given her some cause,' said Cashman.

'He gave her plenty of cause,' said Murphy.

'But they always got on well together.'

'They got on all right,' Murphy admitted. 'But she must have had a terrible life with him. She's a religious girl.'

'Lot's of religious girls marry men like that, though,' said Enright, as though he were following the conversation, which he wasn't.

'Not men like Dick Gordon,' Murphy said broodingly. 'He's an optimist, and optimism is the plague of a religious mind. Dick has no notion how intolerable life can be. A man like that doesn't even believe in Evil.'

3

Dick's optimism was tested severely enough a few years later. He was ill, and word was going round that he would never be well again.

This put half Cork in a flutter, because everyone who had ever had a conversation with him seemed to feel a personal responsibility for seeing that he was converted, and those who might see him were warmly advised of what they should do and say. His boss put a car at the disposal of his friends so that they could rush a priest to his bedside at any hour of the day or night. 'Vultures are a breed of bird that has always fascinated me, though I thought they were supposed to be extinct,' said Ned Murphy. Barbara was exasperated by all the hysteria, more particularly because it put her in such a false position, and her replies became shorter. 'I'm afraid it is a matter I never discuss with my husband,' she said. 'There are certain things that are too personal even for a wife.' Even that did not put people off the subject. They said that converts were never really like their own people.

One rainy evening Dick was alone in the house, trying to read, when a strange priest called. He was tall and fat and very grave.

'Mr Gordon?' he said.

'Yes,' said Dick.

'Can I come in for a moment?'

'Oh, certainly. Sit down.'

'You don't know who I am, Mr Gordon,' the priest said jovially as he took a chair. 'I know quite a lot about you, though. I'm the parish priest, Father Ryan.'

Dick nodded.

'Mr Gordon, I want to talk to you about your soul,' he said with a change of tone.

Dick smiled and lit a cigarette. He had been through it all so often.

'Surely, among your congregation you could find plenty of others,' he suggested mildly.

'Not many in such danger, shall we say,' the priest replied with a smile. Something about the smile shook Dick. It seemed to radiate a sort of cold malice which was new to him.

'Considering that we've only just met, you seem to know a lot about the state of my soul,' Dick said with the same weary sarcasm.

'Mr Gordon,' the priest said, raising his hand, 'I wasn't speaking only of your spiritual danger. Mr Gordon, you're a very sick man.'

Dick rose and opened the door for him.

'Father Ryan, you're concerning yourself with things that have nothing to do with you,' he said icily. 'Now, do you mind getting out of my house?'

'Your arrogance won't last long, Mr Gordon,' the priest said. 'You're dying of cancer.'

'You heard me?' Dick said menacingly.

'You have less than three months to live.'

'All the more reason I shouldn't be persecuted by busybodies like you,' Dick said with sudden anger. 'Now get out before I throw you out.'

He scarcely raised his voice, but anger was so rare with him that it had a sinister quality that overawed the priest.

'You'll regret this,' he said.

'Probably,' Dick said between his teeth. 'I'll regret that I didn't treat you as you deserve.'

Afterwards he went back to his book, but he was even more incapable of reading or of understanding what he read. Something about the priest's tone had upset him. He was himself almost devoid of malice and had shrugged off the opposition to himself as mere foolishness, but this was something more and worse than foolishness. This was foolishness going bad, foolishness turning into named evil. And Dick, as Ned Murphy had said, did not really believe in Evil.

When Barbara came in he was still sitting in darkness before the fire, brooding.

'Hullo, dear,' she said with false brightness. 'All alone?'

'Except for a clerical gentleman who just called,' he said with an air of amusement.

'Oh, dear!' she said in distress. 'Who was it?'

'His name is Ryan. A rather unusual character.'

'What did he want?'

'Oh, just to tell me I had cancer and had less than three months to live,' Dick said bitterly.

'Oh, God, no, Dick! He didn't say that?' she cried, and began to weep.

He looked at her in surprise, and concern and then got up.

'Oh, don't worry about that, Babsy!' he said with a shrug. 'It's only their stock-in-trade you know. You should have heard the pleasure with which he said it! Where would they be without their skeleton to brandish?'

It was only the sort of thing he had said to her in the early days of their marriage and had not said since her conversion. She did not know whether he really meant it or said it just to comfort her. After their years of married life he was still gentle and considerate. His brother, Tom, was little help to her.

'I'll only have to try and be at the house more,' he said gloomily. 'This thing could happen again.'

'But can't we complain to the Bishop about it?' she said angrily.

'I'm afraid that wouldn't do much good, Barbara. The Bishop would be more likely to take Father Ryan's side. By the way, have you confidence in that doctor of yours?'

'Dr Cullen? Oh, I suppose he did what he could.'

'I don't mean that,' Tom said patiently. 'Are you sure he didn't go to Father Ryan himself?'

'Oh, God, Tom!' she said. 'What sort of people are they?'

'Much like people everywhere else, I suppose,' he said despondently.

After this, she dreaded leaving Dick alone. She knew now the hysteria that surrounded them and knew that those who indulged in it were ruthless in a way that Dick would never understand.

One day she was upstairs, chatting with him when the door-bell rang. She answered it and saw Father Hogan outside. He was now parish priest in a village ten miles outside the town, and they saw less of him. He was one of the few friends she had whom Dick seemed to like.

'Come in here, please, Father,' she said, and led him into the little front room. She closed the door and spoke in a low voice. 'Father, I can't have Dick persecuted now.'

'Persecuted?' he asked in surprise. 'Who's persecuting him?'

'You know what he believes,' she said. 'I dare say he's wrong, and if you catch him in a moment of weakness he may say he's wrong, but it will be his weakness, not him.'

'What the hell are you talking about?' he asked angrily. 'Are you out of your mind? I rang him up when I heard he was sick and he asked me to call for a drink. I'm not going to do anything to him – except maybe give him conditional absolution when it's all over, and that won't be on his account. There are people in this town who'd try to refuse him Christian burial. You don't know it, but you wouldn't like it. No more would his family.'

'You had nothing to do with the man who told him he was dying?'

'Why?' he asked quietly. 'Did someone do that?'

'The parish priest did it.'

'And am I to be held responsible for every fool and lout who happens to wear a soutane?' he asked bitterly. 'He asked me in for a drink, Barbara, and I'm going to have it with him, whatever you may think . . .' Then with one of his quick changes of mood he asked, 'Did it upset him?'

'Fortunately, he didn't believe it.'

'Didn't believe it, or pretended not to believe it?' he asked shrewdly and then threw the question away. 'Ah, how would you know? I won't disturb him, Barbara,' he added gently. 'I wish I was as sure of my own salvation as I am of his.'

'So do I – now,' she said, and he knew as though he were inside her that she was regretting the weakness of years before and wishing that she could go into the dark with her husband as they had both imagined it when they were in love. It was the only way that would have meant anything to Dick now. But he was a good priest, and he could not afford to brood on what it all meant. He still had a duty to the living as well as to the friend who was about to die.

(1965)

REQUIEM

FATHER FOGARTY, the curate in Crislough, was sitting by the fire one evening when the housekeeper showed in a frail little woman of sixty or sixty-five. She had a long face, with big eyes that looked as though they had wept a great deal, and her smile lit up only the lower half of her face. Father Fogarty was a young man with a warm welcome for the suffering and the old. A man with emotions cut too big for the scale of his existence, he was for ever floundering in enthusiasms and disillusionments, wranglings and reconciliations; but he had a heart like a house, and almost before the door closed behind her, he was squeezing the old woman's hand in his own two fat ones.

'You're in trouble,' he said in a low voice.

'Wisha, aren't we all, Father?' she replied.

'I'm sorry, I'm sorry,' he said. 'Is it something I can do for you?'

'Only to say Mass for Timmy, Father.'

'I'll do that, to be sure,' he said comfortingly. 'You're cold. Sit down a minute and warm yourself.' Then he laid a big paw on her shoulder and added in a conspiratorial whisper, 'Do you take anything? A drop of sherry, maybe?'

'Ah, don't be putting yourself out, Father.'

'I'm not putting myself out at all. Or maybe you'd sooner a sup of whiskey. I have some damn good whiskey.'

'Wisha, no, Father, I wouldn't, thanks. The whiskey goes to my head.'

'It goes to my own,' he replied cheerfully. 'But the sherry is good, too.' He didn't really know whether it was or not, because he rarely drank, but, being a hospitable man, he liked to give his visitors the best. He poured a glass of sherry for her and a small one for himself, and lit one of his favourite cheroots.

The old woman spread her transparent hands to the blaze and sipped at her wine. 'Oh, isn't the heat lovely?' she exclaimed with girlish delight, showing her old gums. 'And the sherry is lovely, too, Father. Now, I know you're surprised to see me, but I know all about you. They told me to come to you if I was in trouble. And there aren't many priests like that, Father. I was never one to criticize, but I have to say it.'

'Ah,' he said jovially, throwing himself back in his big leather chair and pulling on his cheroot, 'we're like everybody else, ma'am. A mixed lot.'

'I dare say you're right,' she said, 'but they told me I could talk to you.'

'Everyone talks to me,' he said without boastfulness. It was true. There was something about him that invited more confidences than a normal man could respect, and Father Fogarty knew he was often indiscreet. 'It's not your husband?' he added doubtfully.

'Ah, no, Father,' she replied with a wistful smile. 'Poor Jim is dead on me these fifteen years. Not, indeed, that I don't miss him just the same,' she added thoughtfully. 'Sometimes I find myself thinking of him, and he could be in the room with me. No, it's Timmy.'

'The son?'

'No, Father. Though he was like a son to me. I never had any of my own. He was Jim's. One of the last things Jim did was to ask me to look after him, and, indeed, I did my best. I did my best.'

'I'm sure you did, ma'am,' said Father Fogarty, scowling behind his cheroot. He was a man who took death hard, for himself, and for others. A stepchild was not the same thing, of course, but he supposed you could get just as attached to one of those. That was the trouble; you could get attached to anything if only you permitted yourself to do so, and he himself was one who had never known how to keep back. 'I know how hard it is,' he went on, chewing at his cheroot till his left eyebrow descended and seemed to join in the process, and he resembled nothing so much as a film gangster plotting the murder of an innocent victim. 'And there's little anyone can say that will console you. All I know from my own experience is that the more loss we feel the more grateful we should be for whatever it was we had to lose. It means we had something worth grieving for. The ones I'm sorry for are the ones that go through life not even knowing what grief is. And you'd be surprised the number of them you'd meet.'

'I dare say in one way they're lucky,' she said broodingly, looking into the fire.

'They are not lucky, ma'am, and don't you believe it,' he said gruffly. 'They miss all the things that make life worthwhile, without even knowing it. I had a woman in here the other night,' he added, pointing his cheroot at the chair she sat in, 'sitting where you're sitting now, and she told me when her husband gave the last breath she went on her knees by the bed and thanked God for taking him.'

'God help us,' the old woman said, clasping her hands. 'I hope no one does the same thing over herself some day.'

'Thanked God for taking him,' Fogarty repeated with his troubled boyish frown. 'What sort of mind can a woman like that have?'

'Oh, she's hard, she's hard,' agreed the old woman, still looking into the fire.

'Hard as that hearthstone,' he said dramatically. 'My God, a man she'd lived with the best part of her life, whatever his faults might have been! Wouldn't you think at least she'd have some remorse for the things she'd done to him in all those years?'

'Oh, indeed, 'tis true,' she said. 'I often blamed myself over poor Jim. Sometimes I think if only I might have been a bit easier on him, he might be here yet.'

'Most of us have to go through that sooner or later,' he said, feeling that perhaps he had gone too far and reopened old wounds. His own old wounds were never far from breaking open, because often a light or careless word would bring back the memory of his mother and of his diabolical adolescent temperament. 'We have to be careful of that, too,' he added. 'Because it's not the guilty ones who go on brooding, but the others – the people who're only partly guilty, or maybe not guilty at all. That can happen, too. I had a man here last week talking about his wife's death, and nothing I could say would persuade him but that he'd wronged her. And I knew for a fact that he was a husband in a million – a saint. It's something we can't afford to indulge. It turns into a sort of cowardice before life. We have to learn to accept our own limitations as human beings – our selfishness and vanity and bad temper.'

He spoke with passion, the passion of a man teaching a lesson he has never been able to learn himself. Something in his tone made the old woman look at him, and her face softened into a sweet, toothless old smile.

'Haven't you great wisdom for such a young man!' she exclaimed admiringly.

'Great,' he agreed with a jolly laugh. 'I'm the biggest idiot of them all.'

But she shrugged this off. 'Ah, what else were the saints?'

'Look here, ma'am,' he said, rising and standing over her with mock gravity. 'Don't you be going round talking about me as a saint or you'll be having me sent to a punishment parish. The poor Bishop has trouble enough on his hands without having to deal with saints. I'll say eight-o'clock Mass on Sunday for your boy. Will that do you?'

'My boy?' she said in surprise. 'But Timmy wasn't my son, Father. Sure, I said I had no children.'

'No. I took it he was your stepson.'

'Is it Jim's?' she exclaimed with a laugh of genuine amusement at his mistake. 'Ah, sure, Jim wasn't married before,

Father. Don't you see, that's why I had to come to you?'

'I see,' he said, though he didn't, and anyhow he felt it was none of his business. The woman, after all, hadn't come to make her confession. 'What was his surname so?'

'Ah, Father,' she said, still laughing but in a bewildered way, 'I'm so distracted that I can't explain myself properly. You have it all mixed up. Sure, I thought I explained it.'

'You didn't explain it, ma'am,' he said, repressing curiosity. 'And anyway it's nothing to me who Timmy was. That's a matter between you and your confessor.'

'My what?' she cried indignantly. 'Ah, Father, you have me distracted completely now. This has nothing to do with confession. Oh, my, what's that Timmy was? If I could only think!'

'Take your time, ma'am,' he said, but he wondered what was coming next.

'A poodle!' she exclaimed. 'Now I have it.'

'A what?'

'A poodle – a French poodle is what they called him,' she said, delighted to remember the proper term. And then her big eyes began to fill with tears. 'Oh, Father, I don't know how I'm going to get on without him. He was everything to me. The house isn't the same without him.'

'You don't mean you're asking me to say Mass for your *dog*?'

'Oh, I'm not asking you to do it for nothing,' she added with dignity, opening her handbag.

'Are you a Catholic at all, ma'am?' he asked sternly, fixing her with a glowering look that only seemed to amuse her. She tossed her head with a sudden saucy, girlish air.

'Wisha, what else would I be?' she asked gently, and he felt that there was nothing much he could say in reply.

'And do you know what the sacrifice of the Mass is?' he went on.

'Well, as I go every morning of my life, Father, I should have some idea,' she replied, and again he had the feeling that she was laughing at him.

'And don't you know that you're asking me to commit sacrilege? Do you even know what sacrilege is?'

'Ah, what sacrilege?' she exclaimed lightly, shrugging it off. She took three five-pound notes from her old handbag. He knew she intended the money as an offering; he knew it was probably all she had in the world, and he found himself torn between blind rage and admiration.

'Here,' he said. 'Let me get you another drink. And put that blooming money back in your bag or you'll be losing it.'

But the very sound of his voice told him that he was losing conviction. The terrible little old woman with her one idea exercised a sort of fascination over him that almost frightened him. He was afraid that if he wasn't careful he would soon find himself agreeing to do what she wanted. He poured her a drink, threw himself back again in his arm-chair, and at once gave way to his indignation.

'I cannot stand this damn sentimentality!' he shouted, hitting the arm of his chair with his clenched fist. 'Every day of my life I have to see good Christians go without food and fire, clothes and medicine, while the rich people taunt them with the sight of their pampered pets. I tell you I can't stand it!'

'Why, then, I'm sure you're right, Father. But I'm not rich, and no poor person was ever sent away from my door with nothing, as long as I had it.'

'I'm sure of that, ma'am,' he said humbly, ashamed of his outburst. 'I'm sure you're a better Christian than I am, but there are different needs and different duties, and we must not confuse them. There are animal needs and human needs, and human needs and spiritual needs. Your dog has no need of the Mass.'

'He was very fond of Mass. Every morning he came with me and lay down outside the chapel door.'

'And why did you leave him outside the chapel door?' asked Fogarty.

'Why?'

'Yes, why? Wasn't it that you made a distinction between an animal and a spiritual need?'

'It was nothing of the kind,' she said hotly. 'It was the parish priest that asked me, because some old fools complained. Hah, but I often sneaked him in when they weren't looking, and let me tell you, Father, none of those old crawthumpers behaved as devotionally as my Timmy. Up with the Gospel and down at the Elevation, without my saying a word to him. And don't tell me that Our Blessed Lord wasn't as pleased with Timmy as with them.'

'I'm not telling you anything of the sort,' he said, touched and amused. 'All I am telling you is that now that your dog is dead, prayers can make no difference to him. Your dog couldn't incur guilt. Your prayers may make a difference to your husband because, like the rest of us, he did incur guilt in this life and may have to atone for it in the next.'

'Ah, it's easy seen you didn't know Jim, Father. Poor Jim was innocent as a child. He never did anything wrong only taking the little sup of whiskey when I wouldn't be looking. I know he got a bit cranky when he had a drop in and I wouldn't give him any more, but sure that's a thing you wouldn't give a second thought to . . . No, Father,' she added thoughtfully, looking into the fire again, 'I don't mind admitting that the first day or two after he died I wasn't easy in my mind at all. I didn't know what little thing he might have said or done on the side, unknown to me, or what little taste of punishment they might give him. I couldn't rest, thinking of him burning down there in Purgatory, with people he didn't know at all. A shy man, like that, and a man – I won't belie him – that would scream the house down if he as much as got a splinter in his nail. But then I realized that nobody in his right mind could be doing anything to him. Oh, no, Father, that's not why I get Masses said for Jim.'

'Then why do you get them said for him?' Fogarty asked, though he knew the answer. His own big heart answered for him when his reason didn't.

'Sure, what other way have I of letting him know I'm thinking about him?' she asked with a childlike smile. 'He's always in my mind, morning, noon, and night. And now Timmy is the same.'

'And when I tell you that it makes no difference to Timmy – that Timmy can't know he's in your mind?'

'Ah, well, Father, these things are great mysteries,' she replied comfortably, 'and we don't know all about them yet. Oh, I know there's a difference, and I'm not asking for anything impossible. Only one small Mass, so that he'll know. But when I talk to people about it, you'd think I was mad from the way they go on. They tell me he has no soul, because he never committed sin. How does anybody know he didn't commit sin? A little child doesn't commit sin and he has a soul. No, Father,' she went on with iron determination, 'I know I'm old and I have no one to advise me, and my head isn't as good as it was, but thank God I still have my wits about me. Believe me, Father, a dog is no different from a child. When I was feeling low coming on to Jim's anniversary, Timmy would know it. He'd know it as if he could read what I was thinking, and he'd come and put his head on my lap to show how sorry he was. And when he was sick himself, he'd get into my bed and curl up beside me, begging me with his eyes to make him better. Yes, indeed, and when he was dying I felt the same way about him as I felt about poor Jim – just the way you described it, thinking of all the times I was hard on him when he didn't deserve it at all. That is the hardest part of it, Father, when you have to try and forgive yourself.'

'I'm sure you have very little to forgive yourself for, ma'am,' Fogarty said with a smile. 'And God knows, if it was anything I could do for you I'd do it, but this is something that, as a priest, I can't do.'

'And there's no one else I could go to? You don't think if I went to the Bishop myself he'd let you do it?'

'I'm quite certain he wouldn't, ma'am.'

'Ah,' she said bitterly as she raised herself heavily from

her chair, 'if I was younger and smarter with my pen I'd write to the Pope about it myself.' She turned to the door, and Fogarty sprang to open it for her, but the courtesy was lost on her. She looked at him with deep mournful eyes that seemed to contain all the loneliness in the world. 'And it's wrong, Father, wrong,' she said in a firm voice. 'I'm as good a Catholic as the next, but I'd say it to the Pope himself this minute if he walked into this room. They *have* souls, and people are only deluding themselves about it. Anything that can love has a soul. Show me that bad woman that thanked God her husband was dead and I'll show you some-one that maybe hasn't a soul, but don't tell me that my Timmy hadn't one. And I know as I'm standing here that somewhere or other I'll see him again.'

'I hope you do, ma'am,' he said, his big voice suddenly growing gentle and timorous. 'And whenever you say a prayer for him, don't forget to add one for me.'

'I will not indeed, Father,' she said quietly. 'I know you're a good man, and I'll remember you with the others that were good to me, and one of these days, with God's help, we'll all be together again.'

(1957)

VARIATIONS ON A THEME

KATE MAHONEY was sixty when her husband died. After that, she had, like many another widow, to face the loss of her little house. It was a good house in a good lane. There was a sandstone quarry behind, so that no one could overlook them except from a great distance, and though there was a terrace of really superior houses between them and the road, and it had no view and little or no sunlight, it was quiet and free of traffic any hour of the day or night – a lovely place for children, as she often said.

Her two daughters, Nora and Molly, were married, one in Shandon Street and the other on the Douglas Road, but even if either of them had been in a position to offer her a home she would have had doubts about accepting it. What she said was that the people in Shandon Street were uncivilized and the people on the Douglas Road had no nature, but what she really thought was that her daughters shouted too much. The truth was that Kate shouted enough for a regimental sergeant-major, and the girls – both gentle and timid – had learned early in life that the only way of making themselves heard was to shout back. Kate did not shout all the time: she had another tone, reserved for intimate occasions, which was low-pitched and monotonous and in which she tended to break off sentences as though she had forgotten what she was saying. But, low-pitched or loud, her talk was monumental, like headstones. Her hands and legs were twisted with rheumatics, and she had a face like a butcher's block in which the only really attractive feature was the eyes, which looked astonishingly young and merry.

She loved the lane and the neighbours – so different from the nasty strange people you met in Shandon Street and the Douglas Road – but mostly she longed to die in the bed her husband had died in. With the rheumatics she could not go out and do a day's work as other widows did to stretch out their couple of halfpence. It was this that turned her mind to the desperate expedient of taking in a foster-child – this and the realization that the lane was a lovely place for children. She could hardly help feeling that it would be a good influence on a child.

It was a terrible thing to descend to, more particularly for a woman who had brought up two children of her own, but there didn't seem to be any alternative. Motherhood was the only trade she knew. She went with her problem to Miss Hegarty, the nurse, who owned one of the bigger houses between her and the road. Miss Hegarty was a fine-looking woman of good family, but so worn-out by the endless goings-on of the male and female that she admitted to Kate that most of the time she could not be bothered to distinguish between honest and dishonest transactions. 'Aha, Mrs Mahoney!' she said triumphantly. 'They all start out in a laugh and all end up in a cry.' Even to women in labour she would call out joyously, 'Last year's laugh is this year's cry, Mrs Hartnett.' The funny thing about Miss Hegarty was that though nobody had ever mentioned a man's name in connexion with her, she seemed to know of every girl within fifty miles who was in trouble.

Kate, however, found her a good counsellor. She advised her against taking foster-children from the local council because they paid so badly that you would have to take three or four to make a living out of them. The thing to do was to take a child of good family whose mother would be able to support it. Even then you couldn't rely on vagabonds like that because they were all unstable and might skip off to foreign parts without warning, but you would still have the grandparents to fall back on. 'Oh, Mrs Mahoney, if they have it they'll pay to keep their precious daughter's name out of the papers. Fitter for them to keep her off the streets!'

Miss Hegarty knew of a girl of that kind from Limerick who was going to England to have her baby and would probably be glad of a good home for it in Ireland, but not too close to her family. When Mrs Mahoney told Nora and Molly, Molly didn't seem to mind, but Nora got very dramatic and said that personally she'd choose the poorhouse – a remark Kate did not like at all, though it was only what you'd expect from a giddy creature like Nora.

From Nora she borrowed back the old family perambulator, and one spring morning it appeared outside the door in the lane with a baby boy asleep inside, while Kate herself sat on the window-sill to explain her strange position. 'My first!' she shouted gaily, and then went on in the monotonous voice she used for solemn occasions to explain that this was no ordinary child such as you would get from the workhouse, but the son of a beautiful educated girl from one of the wealthiest, best-bred families in Limerick, who herself was manageress of a big shop there. Of course, the neighbours smiled and nodded and groaned, and agreed it was a sad case, but that times were changing; and did not believe a word that Kate told them because they knew a girl like that must have the bad drop, and the bad drop was bound to be passed on. All the same they were sorry for Kate, an old neighbour and a respectable one, who had no choice but to put the best face she could on it. The young married women who, as they said themselves, had paid for their titles, were not so charitable and said that you could not allow decent children to grow up in an atmosphere like that, and that the priest or the landlord should stop it because it was lowering the value of morality and property in the lane. They did not say it too loud, because, however humiliated she might be, Kate was a very obstinate old woman, and a vulgar one as well if she was roused.

So Jimmy Mahoney was permitted to grow up in the lane along with the honest transactions and turned into a good-looking, moody kid, cheerful and quarrelsome, who seemed to see nothing wrong in his mother's being so old. On the contrary, he seemed to depend on her more than the other children did on their real mothers, and sometimes when she left him alone and went off to see Nora or Molly he refused to play and sat and sulked on the doorstep till she got home. Even that ended one day when he simply went after her, without as much as the price of the tram, and walked to the other side of the city to Molly's on the Douglas Road.

'Oh, you divil you!' Kate shouted when she looked round and saw him staring accusingly at her from the front door. 'I thought you were a ghost. A nice position I'd be in if you went and got yourself killed on me!' Then she grinned and said, 'I suppose you couldn't get on without me.' Molly, a beautiful, haggard woman, gave him a smile of mortification and said quietly, 'Come in, Jimmy.' It was a thing she would not have wished for a pound because she knew it would have to be explained to the neighbours as well as her own children. But afterwards, whatever she or Nora might think, Kate brought him with her wherever she went. They might imagine that he had no such claim on their mother, but Jimmy thought otherwise.

But by the time he was five or six things were again going hard with Kate. Money wasn't what it had been and her little margin of profit was contracting. She paid another visit to Miss Hegarty, and this time the nurse had an even more staggering story. It seemed there was this well-to-do girl in Bantry who was engaged to a rich Englishman and then went and had an affair with a married man she had known from the time she was twelve.

'A married man!' exclaimed Kate. 'Oh, my, the things that go on!'

'Don't talk to me, Mrs Mahoney!' Miss Hegarty cried dramatically. 'Don't talk to me. If you knew the half of what was going on, 'twould make you lose your religion.'

Kate felt it her duty to warn Jimmy that he was getting a little brother. Miss Hegarty herself advised that, but whatever Miss Hegarty knew about flighty girls she seemed to know very little about small boys. When Mrs Mahoney told him, he began to roar and kick the furniture till she was sure the whole lane was listening. He said that he didn't want any little brother. He said if she brought one into the house that he'd walk out. He said she was too old to be having babies and that she'd have everyone talking about them. As she sighed afterwards, a husband wouldn't have given her such dogs' abuse. And what Jimmy said was nothing to what her daughters said.

'Ah, Mammy, you're making a holy show of us!' Nora cried when she came to call.

'I'm making a show of ye?' Kate cried wonderingly, pointing at her bosom with the mock-innocent air that maddened her daughters. 'I do my business and I don't cost ye a penny – is that what ye call making a show of ye?'

'Ah, you'd think we were something out of a circus instead of an old respectable family,' stormed Nora. 'That I can hardly face the neighbours when I come up the lane! Ahadie, 'tis well my poor daddy doesn't know what you're making of his little house.' Then she put her hands on her hips like a common market-woman and went on. 'How long do you think you'll be able to keep this up, would you mind us asking? You think you're going to live for ever, I suppose?'

'God is good,' Kate muttered stiffly. 'I might have a few years in me yet.'

'You might,' Nora said mockingly. 'And I suppose you imagine that if anything happens you, Molly and myself will keep up the good work, out of Christian charity?'

'Aha, God help the innocent child that would be depending on Christian charity from the likes of you!' Kate retorted with sudden anger. 'And their people have plenty, lashings of it – more than you'll ever be able to say with your husband in a steady job in the Brewery! How sure you are of yourself! My goodness, that we'd never do anything at all if we were to be always thinking of what was round the next corner. And what about my rent? Are you going to pay it?'

'Ah, 'tisn't the rent with you at all, and it never was,' Nora said with growing fury. 'You only do it because you like it.'

'I like it?' her mother asked feebly, as though she were beginning to doubt Nora's sanity. 'An old woman like me that's crippled with the rheumatics? Oh, my!' she added in a roar of anguish, 'that 'tis in a home I ought to be if I had my rights. In a home!'

'You and your home!' Nora said contemptuously. 'That's enough of your lies now, Mammy! You love it! Love it! And you care more for that little bastard than you ever did about Molly or me.'

'How dare you?' Kate cried, rising with as much dignity as the rheumatics permitted. 'What way is that to speak to your mother? And to talk about a poor defenceless child like that in my house, you dirty, jealous thing! Yes, jealous,' she added in a wondering whisper, as though the truth had only dawned on her in that moment. 'Oh, my! Ye that had everything!'

All the same, Kate was a bit shaken, not because of the row, because the Mahoneys had always quarrelled like that, as though they all suffered from congenital deafness, and they got the same pleasure out of the mere volume of sound they could produce that certain conductors get out of Wagner. What really mortified her was that she had given herself away in front of Nora, whose intelligence she despised. Now if it had been Molly she wouldn't have minded so much, for though Molly was apparently serving her time to be a saint, she had the intelligence to see through Kate's little dodges. It was true that Kate had taken Jimmy in for perfectly good mercenary reasons, and that without him she would have no home at all; and it was very wrong under the circumstances for Nora to impute sentimental motives to her; but all the same she wasn't so far wrong. Motherhood was the only trade Kate knew, and she liked to practise it as her poor husband had liked to make little chairs and tables in the last year of his life, when no one cared whether he made them or not; and though her rheumatics were bad and her sight wasn't all it used to be, she felt she practised it better the older she got. It was also true enough to say that she enjoyed Jimmy more than she had enjoyed her own children, and if you had pressed her about it she would have said that in those days she had been young and worried about everything. But if you had pressed her hard enough, you would also have discovered that there wasn't a boy in the whole road that she thought was a patch on Jimmy. And what was wrong with that? she might have added. You might say what you like but there was a lot in good blood.

She would not have understood at all if you had accused her of being an old dreamer who was attracted to Jimmy by the romance and mystery of his birth – the sort of thing she had missed in her own sober and industrious youth, but, just the same, Jimmy gave her the chance of sitting over the fire in the evening with some old crony and discussing like a schoolgirl things she would scarcely have known existed.

'Oh, when I seen Jimmy's mother that day in the solicitor's office she was like something you'd see in a shop window, Mrs Sumners,' she would chant. 'She was beautiful, beautiful! And I could see by that set face of hers that she had a month of crying all bottled up inside her. Oh, Mrs Sumners, if you seen her the way I did you'd know that nothing she could do would be bad.'

And later, when she had tucked Jimmy in for the night and lay awake in the other room, saying her rosary, she would often forget her prayers and imagine how she would feel if one stormy night (for some reason she made it stormy) there came a knock to the door and Kate saw Jimmy's father standing in the lane, tall and handsome with a small black moustache and the tears in his eyes. 'Mr Mulvany,' she would say to the teacher (she was always making up names and occupations for Jimmy's unknown father), 'your son wants nothing from you,' or (if she was in a generous mood), 'Senator MacDunphy, come in. Jimmy was beginning to think you'd never find him.'

But dreamers are for ever running into degrading practicalities that they have failed to anticipate, and there was one thing about her extraordinary family that really worried Kate. Before she had even laid eyes on him, the second boy had also been christened James, and because she was terrified of everything to do with the law she did not dare to change his name. But so that Jimmy should not be too upset, she left his name as it was, plain James – an unnatural name for any child as she well knew.

James was a very different sort of child from Jimmy. He was a baby with a big head, a gaping mouth, and a cheerless countenance that rarely lit up in a smile. Even from the first day it was as though he knew he was there only on sufferance and resigned himself to the fact.

Fortunately, Jimmy took to him at once. He liked being left in charge, and was perfectly happy to change and entertain him. He explored the neighbourhood to study all the other babies and told Kate that James was cleverer than the whole lot of them. He even got Kate's permission to wheel the old perambulator up and down the main road so that people could see for themselves what James was like and came back with great satisfaction to report any approving remarks he happened to elicit. As he had a violent temper and would fight anyone up to twice his weight, the other kids did not make any public remarks about this sissified conduct.

2

A couple of times a year Jimmy's mother, whom he knew only as Aunt Nance, came to stay with friends in Cork, and Jimmy visited her there and played with the two children, who were called Rory and Mary. He did not like Rory and

Mary because they ganged up on him at once, and he only went on his aunt's account. She was tall and good-looking with a dark complexion and dark, dark hair; she talked in a crisp nervous way, and was always forgetting herself and saying dirty words like 'Cripes!' and 'Damn!' which delighted Jimmy because these were words that were supposed to be known only to fellows.

When he got home, Kate asked him all sorts of questions about his visit, like how many rooms there were in the house, what he ate there, what sort of furniture there was and what size was the garden – things that never interested Jimmy in the least.

When James began to grow up, he too asked questions. He wanted to know what school Rory and Mary went to, what they learned there, and whether or not Mary played the piano. These were questions that did not interest Jimmy, but it dawned on him that James was lonely when he was left behind like that and wanted to see the Martins' place for himself. It seemed an excellent idea to Jimmy, because James was a steady, quiet kid who would get on much better with Rory and Mary than he did, but when he suggested it Kate only said James was too young and Aunt Nance said she'd see.

It ended by his suspecting that there was something fishy about James. There had always been something fishy about him, as though he didn't really belong to the family. Jimmy wasn't clear how you came to belong to the family, but he knew it had to happen in a hospital or in the house, and he couldn't remember anything of the sort happening to James. One evening, when Kate was complaining of her rheumatics, he asked her casually if she hadn't gone to hospital with it.

'Ah, how would the likes of me go to hospital?' she asked sourly. 'I was never in a hospital in my life and I hope I never am.'

James was in the room, and Jimmy said no more for the time being. Later that night he returned to the subject.

'You're not James' mother, are you, Mammy?'

'What's that you say?' she cried in astonishment.

'I said you're not James' mother, that's all.'

'Oye, what queer things you think of!' she said crossly.

'But you're not,' he said with a shrug. 'You only too
him in because his own mother didn't want him, isn't tha
it?'

'You inquisitive puppy!' she hissed. 'Don't let the chil
hear you saying things like that.'

'But it's true, isn't it? She's the one you get the mone
from.'

Kate threatened him into silence, but she was terrifie
'Oh, my, the cunning of him!' she said next day to Mr
Sumners. 'The way he cross-hackled me – that poor Jac
Mahoney never did the like all the long years we were ma
ried! And what am I to say to him? Who will I get to advis
me?' The neighbours could not advise her, and even if the
tried it would be useless, because they had no more exper
ence than herself. Miss Hegarty might have been able
advise her, but Kate felt that asking her advice would be
sort of admission that she had failed in the job.

And all the time Jimmy's behaviour grew worse. At th
best of times it wasn't very good. Though occasionally h
got into high spirits and entertained herself and James by th
hour, telling funny stories, the high spirits rarely laste
long, and he sulked on his bed with a comic. After this h
would go out with other, rougher kids, and return late wit
a guilty air she could spot from the end of the lane, an
which meant he had broken a window or stolen somethin
from a shop. She watched him from the back door when sh
saw him in the quarry, because she was sure he had a hide
hole there where he kept the things he stole, but when sh
poked round there by herself she could never find anythin
At times like these she was never free of anxiety, becaus
she knew it imperilled the sufferance the neighbours ex
tended to him, and if ever a policeman – which God forbi
– came to her door, they would be the first to say it was a

you could expect of a boy like that. But this was the worst bout yet.

Finally, she decided to tell him the truth about James, or as much of it as she thought he could understand, and one night when James was asleep she sat with him in the darkness over the kitchen fire and told him in her monotonous voice about this beautiful, beautiful girl in Bantry and how as a girl she was in love with this nice young man, and his cruel parents made him marry a girl he did not love at all, and then the girl's parents persuaded her to marry this rich Englishman with motor-cars and yachts and big houses in all parts of the world, but at the last moment the poor girl's heart misgave her and she tried to be reunited to the one she truly loved. She told it so movingly that by the end she was in tears herself, but Jimmy's first words startled her out of her daydream.

'All the same, Mammy, James should be with his own mother,' he said.

She was astonished and dismayed at the maturity of his tone. This was no longer any of the Jimmys she had known, but one who spoke with the sort of authority poor Jack had exercised on the odd occasions when he called his family to order. She even found herself apologizing in the way she might have apologized to poor Jack.

'Ah, wisha, how could she without that husband of hers knowing?'

'Then she ought to tell him,' Jimmy said, and again it was like her dead husband's voice speaking to her.

'Tell him? Tell him what?'

'Everything.'

'Is it to be upsetting the child?' she asked complainingly.

'If she doesn't upset him, somebody else will,' he said with his brooding, old-mannish air.

'They will, they will, God help us!' she sighed. 'People are bad enough for anything. But the poor child may as well be happy while he can.'

But it was Jimmy, not James, she was concerned about. James might get by, a colourless, studious, obedient boy like him, without giving much offence to anyone, but one day Jimmy would beat another boy or steal something from a shop and the whole truth would come out. For a few moments she was tempted to tell him, but she was afraid of what his mother would say when she knew.

Meanwhile, she saw to her surprise that she seemed to have given Jimmy a purpose in life, though it was something she might have expected. Jimmy was always like that, up or down, full of initiative and independence or shiftless and dependent. Now he took over James personally. He announced that it was bad for the kid to be so much alone and took him with him when he went down the Glen or up the river with bigger boys. It was not James' notion; he didn't like bigger boys and didn't in the least mind being left alone with the bits of clean paper he managed to pick up for his writings and drawings, but Jimmy said it was for his good and anything anyone said was good for James he would give a fair trial to. When he came home he repeated his adventures to Kate in the literal gloomy manner of a policeman making a report.

'Jimmy took me down the Glen with Bobby Stephens and Ted Murtagh. I don't like Ted Murtagh. He says dirty words. Jimmy and me fished for thorneybacks. Then he showed me a blackbird's nest. You can't touch a bird's nest because the bird would know and leave the young ones to die. Ted Murtagh robs birds' nests. I think that's wrong, don't you, Mammy?'

James collected bits of information, right and wrong, apparently under the impression that they would all come in handy one day, and to each of them he managed to attach a useful moral lesson. No wonder he sometimes made Jimmy smile.

But Jimmy still continued to brood on James' future. He waited until Aunt Nance came to Cork again, and when he got her to himself he poured it all out on her. He had manged to convince himself that Kate had not understood, but that Aunt Nance who was cleverer would only have to hear the facts to do something about it. Before he had even finished the story she gave him a queer hurt look and cut him off.

'You'll know what it's all about one of these days,' she said.

'But don't you think he should be with his mother?' he asked.

'I don't know,' she said with her boldest air, and then took out a cigarette. 'And even if I did, I wouldn't criticize,' she added.

'Well, I think it's wrong,' he said sullenly. 'The poor kid has no one to play with. Couldn't I bring him over here tomorrow?'

'Begod, you couldn't, Jimmy,' she said. 'Too many blooming kids they have on this place already, if you ask me.'

He left her in one of his mutinous, incoherent fits of rage. He did not take the bus home, even though he had the money, but walked and stood on the river's edge, flinging stones. It was late when he got home, but he told Kate the whole story. 'Ah, what business have you to be interfering?' he asked miserably. He went to bed, and she heard him tossing and muttering to himself. Finally she lit the candle and went into the little attic room that he shared with James. He sat up in bed and looked at her with mad eyes.

'Go away!' he whispered fiercely. 'You're not my mother at all.'

'Oye!' she whimpered, sleepy and scared. 'You and your mother!'

'You're not, you're not, you're not!' he muttered. 'I know all now. I'm like James, only you wouldn't tell me. You haven't the decency. You tell me nothing only lies.'

'Whisht, whisht, whisht, and don't wake the child!' she whispered impatiently. 'Come into the other room.'

He stumbled out ahead of her in his nightshirt, and she sat on the edge of her bed and put her arm round him. He was

shivering as if he had a fever, and she no longer felt capabl
of controlling the situation. She felt old and tired and be
trayed.

'What made you think of it, child?' she asked wearily.

'Aunt Nance,' he said with a sob.

'Was it she told you?' She knew she didn't even soun
surprised.

'No. She wouldn't tell me anything, only I saw she wa
afraid.'

'Who was she afraid of?'

'I asked her to get James' mother to bring him home witl
her and she got frightened.'

'Oh, oh, oh, you poor desolate child, and you only did i
for the best!' she wailed.

'I want to know who my mother is,' he cried despairingly
'Is it Aunt Kitty?' (Kitty was the mother of Rory an
Mary.)

'Why then, indeed, it is not.'

'Is it Aunt Nance so?'

'Wisha, child, lie down here and you can sleep witl
Mammy.'

'I don't want to sleep,' he said frantically. 'How can
sleep? I want to know who my mother is, and you won't te
me.' Then, turning suddenly into a baby again, he put hi
head on her lap and wept. She patted his fat bottom unde
his nightshirt and sighed. 'You're perished,' she said. 'Wha
am I going to do with you?' Then she lifted him into her be
and pulled up the clothes.

'Will I get you a cup of tea?' she asked with feigne
brightness, and, as he shook his head, she added, 'I will,
will.' A cup of tea in the middle of the night was the greates
luxury she could think of. She put on an old coat and wen
downstairs to the kitchen where the oil lamp was turne
low. There was still a spark of fire left and she blew on it an
boiled the big iron kettle. When she climbed awkwardl
back up the stairs with the two mugs of tea she heard hir
still sobbing and stopped. 'God direct me!' she said aloud

Then she sat on the edge of the bed and shook him. 'Drink this, my old *putog*!' she said humorously. It had always made him laugh to be called a sausage.

'I don't want it,' he said. 'I want to know who my mother is.'

'Drink it, you dirty little caffler!' she said angrily. 'Drink it or I won't tell you at all.'

He raised himself in the bed and she held the mug to his mouth, but he could not stop shivering and the tea spilled over his nightshirt and the bedclothes. 'My good sheet!' she muttered. Then she took her own cup and looked away into a corner of the room as though to avoid his eyes. 'She is your mother, your Aunt Nance,' she said in a harsh, expressionless voice, 'and a good mother she is, and a good woman as well, and it will be a bad day for you when you talk against her or let anyone else do it. She had the misfortune to meet a man that was beneath her. She was innocent. He took advantage of her. She wasn't the first and she won't be the last.'

'Who was it?' he asked.

'I don't know, and I don't want to know.'

'Who was it? Because I'm going to find out and when I do I'm going to kill him.'

'Why then, indeed, you're going to do nothing of the sort,' she said sharply. 'He's your father, and he's there inside you, and the thing you will slight in yourself will be the rock you'll perish on.'

The dawn came in the window, and she still rambled on, half dead with sleep. Later, when she reported it to her cronies, she said with a sour laugh that it was nothing but lies from beginning to end, and what other way could it be when she hadn't a notion how a girl like that would feel, but at the time it did not seem to be lies. It seemed rather as though she were reporting a complete truth that was known only to herself and God. And in a queer way it steadied Jimmy. The little man came out in him again. Once she had persuaded him of the truth of his mother's being a victim, he had no further thought for his own trouble.

'Mammy, why didn't she bring me to live with her?' he asked earnestly. 'I could look after her.'

'Oye, you will, child, you will one of these days,' she said sourly. Though later it seemed funny to think of Jimmy looking after his mother, at the time it only hurt her because she would never have a son who would feel that way about her. Daughters were a poor thing for a mother to be relying on.

'Mammy, does this mean that there's something wrong with James and me?' he asked at last, and she knew that this was the question that preoccupied him above all others.

'Indeed, it means nothing of the sort,' she cried, and for the first time it seemed to herself that she was answering in her own person. 'It is nothing. Only bad, jealous people would say the likes of that. Oh, you'll meet them, never fear,' she said, joining her hands, 'the scum of the earth with their marriage lines and their baptismal lines, looking down on their betters! But mark what I say, child, don't let any of them try and persuade you that you're not as good as them. And better! A thousand times better!'

Strange notions from a respectable old woman who had never even believed in love!

3

When Jimmy was fourteen and James between eight and nine, Jimmy's mother decided it was time for him to come and live with her. At first things seemed to have turned out well for her. After Jimmy's birth she had met a very nice young man who fell in love with her. She had told him the whole story, and unlike the general run of fellows in her neighbourhood, who sheered away from her the moment they caught a whiff of scandal, he accepted it as a normal event that might have happened to any decent girl. This seemed to her much too good to be true, and she had held off marrying him for years. The irony of it was that when she knew he was really in love with her and she with him, it was too late. After long years of marriage they had no children of their own. Even before this became obvious he had wanted to adopt Jimmy and bring him up as their own child, but she had put it off and off. First, she said, she wanted them to have the pleasure of a normal child in normal surroundings; Jimmy would come later. But now there was little chance of that, and she had begun to blame herself, to feel, even, that it was a sort of judgement on her for having given Jimmy up originally. Finally, her husband had laid down the law. They were having Jimmy to live with them and the neighbours could say what they pleased.

It was a terrible shock to Kate, though why it should have been she didn't know, since for years it was she who had argued with her neighbours that the time had come for Jimmy to have a proper education and mix with the right class of people. Now she realized that she was just as jealous and possessive as anyone else. She had never criticized Jimmy's mother or allowed anyone else to do so, but now she hadn't a good word to say for her. 'She neglected him when it suited her, and now when it suits her she wants him back,' she complained to Mrs Sumners. 'Ah, now you have to be fair, ma'am,' Mrs Sumners, replied philosophically. 'Fair? Why have I to be fair?' Kate retorted angrily. 'Let them that have it be fair. Them that are without it are entitled to their say.'

Besides, Jimmy provoked her. He was always up or down, and now he was up all the time, thinking only of the marvellous new world that was opening before him and without a thought for herself and James. He told her blithely that he would always come back for the holidays and comforted James by saying that his turn would come next and he'd be going to London. 'He will, he will,' she said and began to weep. 'And neither of ye will care what happens to me.' At this he grew frantic and shouted, 'All right, I won't go if you don't want me to.' Then she turned the full force of her malice on him and shouted, 'Who said I didn't want you to go? How could I keep you here, and me with nothing? Go to the ones with the cars and the fur coats! Go to the ones that can look after you!'

And yet when his stepfather came and took him away she had a feeling of immense relief. She realized that she was not the one to look after him. He was too wild; too big and noisy and exacting; he needed a man to keep him in order, and besides, now that she had become old and stiff and half blind, the housekeeping was more of a strain. She would decide to give herself and James a treat and go to town for the good stewing beef, and suddenly realize when she got back to the house that she had forgotten how to make stew. 'God direct me!' she would say aloud, closing her eyes. 'How was it I used to make it when I was younger? "Delicious" poor Jack used to say it was.'

James was an easier proposition altogether, a boy who wouldn't notice whether you gave him stew or a can of soup or a mug of tea so long as he got the occasional penny for his exercise books. It was music with him now, and he spent hours carefully ruling over the exercise books and making marks that he said were operas and singing them over to her in a tuneless sort of voice. Signs on it, he had almost ruined his eyes and she had to get black glasses for him. He was having trouble in school as well, for the headmaster, who lived up the road, knew who he was and disliked having such a boy in his good clean Catholic school.

One day James came home and said in his unemotional way, 'Mammy, Mr Clancy said to me today, "James Mahoney, or whatever your name is." I don't think it was very nice of him to say that, Mammy, do you?' Kate went a little mad. Her first notion was to complain Mr Clancy to the Dean, but she had a suspicion that the Dean and Clancy were hand-in-glove and that any justice she got she would have to take for herself. So she donned her old hat and coat, took her umbrella by way of a walking-stick and went up the road to the headmaster's big house. When he appeared at the door, she asked him what he meant by insulting her child, and he called her 'an impudent old woman' and slammed the door in her face. Then she banged on the knocker, beat the door with the handle of her umbrella, and read and spelt him for two generations back. She saw by the way that the curtains along the road were being twitched that she had an audience, and she recounted how his mother, known to the Coal Quay as 'Norry Dance Naked', had owned slum property and refused to supply doors for the conveniences. It must be admitted that she was a very vulgar old woman, and after that James had to go to the monks. The monks did not mind who his mother was, because they soon satisfied themselves that James was a born examination-passer who was worth good money to them.

But the loss of Jimmy showed her how precarious was her hold on James, and in the evenings when they were alone she encouraged him to talk about what he would do when he was grown up. James, it seemed to her, had only one ambition, and that was to become a statue. He knew all the statues in town, and for a while had been rather depressed because it had seemed to him that the only way to become a statue was to be a martyr for Ireland, a temperance reformer, or the founder of a religious order, none of which attracted him. But then he discovered from a library book that you could also be a statue for writing books or composing music, which was why he worked so hard making up operas. Looking at his big solemn face in the firelight, Kate thought that there was something of the statue about it already.

Jimmy had been a great boy to raise a laugh, particularly against himself, and James, who knew the way she felt about him, tried to be funny too; but if she was to be killed for it, she could not raise a laugh at James' jokes. And yet she knew that James was gentler, steadier, and more considerate. 'Jimmy have the fire, but James have the character' was how she summed them up.

Then early one morning she heard a hammering on the front door and started up in panic, feeling sure something had happened to Jimmy. He had been on her mind for a week, and she had been scolding James to stop blinding himself over his old books and write to his brother to see was he all right. It was a queer way for a woman to behave who had been congratulating herself on having got rid of him, but Kate's mental processes were never very logical. Without even waiting to ask who was there she opened the door and saw Jimmy outside. Instantly she was lightheaded with relief and joy.

'Oh, child, child!' she sobbed, throwing her arms round his neck. 'Sure, I thought you'd never come home. How did you get here at all?'

'I walked most of it,' he said with a characteristic dash of boastfulness.

'You did, you did, you divil you, you did!' she muttered impatiently and then her voice rose to a squeal of anguish. 'Are them your good trousers?'

'Who is it, Mammy?' James shouted petulantly from upstairs.

'Come down and see, can't you?' she retorted, and went to tinker with the fire while James came downstairs in his nightshirt.

'Sorry I'm back, James?' Jimmy said with a grin, holding out his hand.

'No, Jimmy, I'm very glad you're back,' James said in a small voice.

'Put on your topcoat, you little devil!' cried Kate. 'How often have I to be telling you not to go round in your shirt? Out to the yard, and everything . . . That fellow!' she sighed to Jimmy. 'He have the heart scalded in me. I'd want ten eyes and hands, picking things up after him.'

They had breakfast together just as the sun was beginning to pick out the red quarry behind the house, and it tinged Jimmy's face with fresh colour as he told them of his all-night trip. It was a marvel to Kate how she had managed to listen to James all that time, remembering how Jimmy could tell a story. Whatever James told you always seemed to begin or end with something like 'Mammy, wasn't I clever?', but Jimmy began by revealing himself a fool and ended by suggesting something worse, but it never crossed your mind that he was a fool at all.

'And what did you do with the money for the fare?' Kate asked suspiciously. 'Spent it, I suppose?'

'What fare?' he asked, blushing.

'I suppose she gave you the money for the train at any rate?'

'Oh, I didn't tell her.'

'You didn't what?' Kate asked slowly. 'Oh, my! I suppose you had a fight with her and then walked out of the house without a word to her or anybody? I declare to God you're never right.'

'She doesn't mind what I do,' Jimmy said with a defiant shrug.

'She doesn't, I hear!' Kate said ironically. 'I suppose she didn't pay you enough attention? And now she'll be blaming it all on me. She'll be saying I have you ruined. And she'll be right. I have you ruined, you little caffler!' She opened the back door and looked up at the great sandstone face of the quarry reflecting the morning light. 'Oh, my! There's a beautiful morning, glory be to God!'

A half an hour later she heard the unfamiliar sound of a car turning into the lane and cocked her head in alarm. It stopped immediately in front of the cottage. She spun round on Jimmy, who was now as white as she felt herself. 'Is that the police?' she asked in an angry whisper. She knew it was the wrong thing to say, but Jimmy did not appear to hear her. All the glow seemed to have gone out of him. 'If that's Uncle Tim I'm not going back with him,' he said dully. Kate went to the front door and saw Nance's husband, a good-looking young man with the sort of pink-and-white complexion she called 'delicate'.

'Here we are again, Mrs Mahoney,' he said without rancour.

'Oh, come in, sir, come in,' she said obsequiously, wiping her hands in her sack apron, and now she was no longer the proud, possessive mother, but the old hireling caught in possession of property that was not rightly hers. The young man strode into the kitchen as if it was his own and stopped dead when he saw Jimmy sitting by the window.

'Now, what made me come here first?' he asked goodnaturedly. 'Mrs Mahoney, I have the makings of a first-class detective in me. Tim the Tracer, that's my name. Criminals shudder when they hear it.' When Jimmy said nothing he cocked his head reproachfully. 'Well, Jimmy?' he asked. Kate could see that Jimmy both liked and dreaded him.

'I'm not going back with you, Uncle Tim,' he said with an indignation that was half an appeal.

'Begor, you are, Jimmy,' his stepfather said, but still with no trace of resentment. 'It wouldn't be much use me going back to Limerick without you. And if you think I'm going to spend the rest of my days chasing you round Ireland, you're wrong. This last jaunt was enough for me.' He sat down, and Kate saw he was exhausted.

'Wisha, you'll have a cup of tea,' she said.

'I will, and a whole teapot-full, Mrs Mahoney,' he replied. 'I didn't even have time to get my breakfast with this fellow.'

'I don't want to go back, Uncle Tim,' Jimmy said furiously. 'I want to stop here.'

'Listen to that, ma'am,' Tim said, cocking his head at Kate. 'Insulting Limerick, and in Cork of all places!'

'I'm not saying anything about Limerick,' Jimmy cried despairingly, and again he was a child and defenceless against the dialectic of adults. 'I want to stop here.'

Screwing up her eyes as she filled the teapot again and put it on the table, Kate tried to intervene on his behalf.

'Wisha, 'tis only a little holiday he wants, sir,' she said humbly, but this only made Jimmy madder than ever.

'It isn't a holiday I want,' he shouted. 'I want to stop here for good. This is my home, and I told my mother so.'

'And don't you think that was a pretty hard thing to say to your mother, Jimmy?' his stepfather asked dryly.

'It's true,' Jimmy said angrily.

'Come on and have your cup of tea, sir,' Kate said, trying to smooth things down. 'Will you have another, Jimmy?'

'I will not,' Jimmy said, beginning to cry. 'And it isn't that I'm not fond of her, but she left it too late. She shouldn't have left it so late, Uncle Tim.'

'You might be right there, son,' his stepfather said wearily, pulling his chair up to the table. 'You can let things like that go too far, and maybe you are too old to get used to your mother. But you're not going the right way about it either.'

'All right then,' Jimmy cried, at the end of his tether. 'What should I do?'

'Don't run out of a situation whenever it gets too hard,' his stepfather said, going on with his skimpy breakfast of bread and tea. 'People's feelings are hurt when you do things like that. Talk to her and tell her how you feel. Maybe the best thing would be for you to come back and go to a proper school here, but leave it to her to make the arrangements. You see, you don't seem to understand what it cost your mother to bring you home at all. It may have been the wrong thing to do; it may have been a failure, but you don't want to leave her feeling that her life is nothing but failures.'

'He's right, Jimmy, boy, he's right,' Kate said, recognizing the deep feeling in his tone. 'If you don't go back now you could never go back with all the old talk there would be. But if you go back now, you can always go home for the holidays.'

'Oh, all right,' Jimmy said with despair.

And it was real despair as she well knew, not play-acting. Of course, he indulged in a bit of that as well. He would not kiss her when he was leaving, and when James said cheerfully, 'You'll be back with us in a couple of weeks', Jimmy took a deep breath and said, 'I may or I may not', leaving it to be understood that he did not rule out the possibility of suicide. But she knew that he did not want to go, that he looked on her house as the only home he knew, and she had great boasting about it among the neighbours. 'A boy of fourteen, ma'am, that was never away from home all the days of his life, travelling back like that through the night, without food or sleep – oh, my, where would you find the likes of him?'

And at the end of his stay with his mother they resumed their existence together more or less where it had been broken off. There was only one major change in their relationship. A couple of days after his return Jimmy said, 'I'm not going to call you "Mammy" any more.' 'Oye, and what are you going to call me?' she asked with sour humour. 'I'm going to call you "Granny",' he said. 'The other sounds too silly.' After a few weeks, James, who had continued to call her by the old name, said 'Granny' too, as though by mistake, and she suddenly lost her temper and flew at him. 'Glad enough you were of someone to call "Mammy"!' she shouted. Though she knew it was only fair, she did not like it. Like the young married women who had objected to Jimmy and himself in the first place, she felt she had paid for her title.

4

A year later, what with the rheumatics and the bronchitis, Kate had to go to hospital, and Nora and Molly each agreed to take one of the boys, but when it was put up to them neither of them would agree. They stayed on in the little house by themselves, and each week one of the girls came up a couple of times to clear up after them. They reported that the mess was frightful, though you could always tell which of the boys was responsible, because Jimmy was a conscientious messer, who piled everything into one enormous heap, apparently in the hope that Santa Claus would find it, while James left things wherever he happened to be whenever an idea struck him. As a result Kate left hospital too soon, but even then she was too late to prevent mischief, for while she was away Jimmy had quietly left school and got himself a job in a packers.

'Oh, you blackguard!' she sighed fondly. 'I knew you'd be up to something the minute my back was turned. Oh, my, that I'd want a hundred eyes! But back to school you go tomorrow, my fine gentleman, if I have to drag you there myself. And 'twouldn't be the first time.'

'How can I go back to school?' Jimmy asked indignantly. They could have the law on me unless I gave a month's notice.' Jimmy knew that she was terrified of policemen, lawyers, and inspectors, and even at her advanced age was always in dread of being marched off to jail for some crime she never committed.

'I'll talk to the manager myself,' she said. 'Who is he?'

'You can't talk to the manager,' said Jimmy. 'He's away on holidays.'

'Oh, you liar!' she muttered happily. 'There's no end to the lies you tell. Who is it, you scamp?'

'Anyway, I have to have a job,' Jimmy said in a grown-up voice. 'If anything happens to you, who's going to look after James?'

'Oh, you divil out of hell!' she said, because it was something that had worried her a lot, and she knew now that Jimmy realized it. But at the same time she knew that Jimmy was the sort of bossy kid who would take on a responsibility like that because he could show off about it, but he would have his own good reasons, which you wouldn't see until later.

'A lot he have to hope for if 'tis you he's relying on!' she shouted. 'Did you tell your mother?'

'That's right,' he said bitterly, confounded by her injustice. What time have I to write to my mother?'

'Plenty of time you have to write to her when 'tis money you want,' Kate said with a knowing air. 'Sit down there and write to her now, you vagabond! I suppose you want me to take the blame for your blackguarding.'

Jimmy with his usual martyred air sat at the table and agonized over a note to his mother.

'How do you spell "employment", James?' he asked.

'Aha!' she exclaimed malevolently. 'He wants to give up school and he don't know how to spell a simple word.'

'All right, spell it you, so!' he retorted.

'In my time, for poor people, the education was not going,' she replied with great dignity. 'People hadn't the chances they have now, and what chances they had, they respected, not like the ones that are going today. Go on with your letter, you thing!'

And again his stepfather came and argued with him. He explained patiently that without a secondary education of some sort Jimmy would never get into a college and would probably never rise above being a common labourer. Jimmy knew his stepfather liked him and began to cry, but he was in one of his obstinate moods and would not give in. He said again and again that he wanted to be independent. When his stepfather left, he accompanied him to the car, and they had a long conversation that made Kate suspicious.

'What were ye talking about?' she asked.

'Oh, nothing,' Jimmy said lightly. 'I only asked him who my father was. He says he doesn't know.'

'And if he says it, he means it,' snapped Kate. 'How inquisitive you're getting.'

'He said I was entitled to know,' Jimmy replied angrily. 'He told me I should ask Nance.' (Sometimes he called his mother 'Mother' and sometimes 'Nance', and whichever he said sounded awkward.)

'You should,' Kate said ironically. 'I'm sure she's dying to tell you.'

But when next he came back from a visit to his mother he had a triumphant air, and late in the evening he said boastfully, 'Well, I found out who my father was anyway.'

'It didn't take you long,' said Kate. 'How did you do it?'

'It was Uncle Tim, really,' he admitted. 'I was arguing with Nance when he walked in. He was mad! He just said,

"Get out, Jimmy!" and I did. Half an hour later he came into me and said, "Now go and talk to your mother!" She was crying.'

'Small wonder!' Kate said with a shrug. 'Who was it?'

'Nobody in particular, actually,' Jimmy admitted with a defeated air. 'The name was Creedon. He had some sort of grocery shop in North Cork, but he's left that for years. She thinks he's in Birmingham, but I'm going to find out.'

'For what?' she asked. 'What good will it do you to find out?'

'I can go to see him, can't I?' he asked defiantly.

'You can what?'

'Go and see him,' he grumbled with some doubt in his voice. 'Why wouldn't I?'

'Why wouldn't you, indeed, and all the attention he paid you!' she retorted. 'You're never right.'

And, indeed, there were times when she thought he wasn't. For months on end he seemed not to think at all of his parentage, and then he began to daydream till he worked himself into a fever of emotion. In a fit like that she never knew what he might do. He was capable of anything, and even though it might never come to violence, she did not know from day to day what deep and irreparable hurt some casual remark might inflict on him.

One day he went off. A sailor on the Fishguard boat had arranged for him to travel free. While he was away she fretted, and, of course, being Jimmy, he did not even send a card to say where he was. She nursed the vague hope that Jimmy would not be able to locate his father; that he would have moved; but, knowing Jimmy's obstinacy in pursuit of an obsession, she had little confidence in this. She tried to imagine what their meeting would be like and hoped only that his father would not say anything to provoke him.

'Oh, my!' she sighed to James. 'If Jimmy took it into his head, he'd kill him.'

'Oh, no, Granny!' James said in his bored way. 'Jimmy

isn't going to England just to kill him. He has more sense than you think.'

'Oye, and what is he going for?' she asked. 'Since you know so much about him?'

'It's only curiosity,' James said. 'Jimmy is always looking for something that was never there.'

Then, one autumn morning, after James had left for school at the other side of the city, Jimmy walked in, looking dirty and dishevelled. He had had no breakfast, and she fumbled blindly about the kitchen, trying to get it for him in a hurry, and cursing old age that made it such a labour. But her heart was light. She had only been deceiving herself, thinking that Jimmy and his father might quarrel, when all that could have happened that would have made a difference to her was that they might have got on too well.

'Oh, you blackguard!' she said fondly, leaning on the kitchen table and grinning into his face, to see him better. 'Where were you?'

'Everywhere.'

'And did you find him?'

'Of course I found him. I had to follow him to London.'

'And what do you think of him now you have him?' she asked, too jovially to be true.

'Ah, he's all right,' Jimmy said casually, and his tone didn't sound true either. 'I don't think he has long to live though. He's drinking himself to death.'

Instantly she was ashamed of her own jealousy and pettiness – she could afford to be, now that she had him back.

'Ah, child, child, why do you be upsetting yourself about them?' she cried miserably. 'They're not worth it. Nobody is worth it.'

She sat in the kitchen with him for two hours. It was just as when he had run away from his mother's house, as though he had been saving it all up for her – the tramp across Wales and England, the people who had given him lifts, and

e lorry-driver who had given him dinner and five bob
hen Jimmy had told his story. She felt she could see it all,
ven the scene when he knocked at the door in the shabby
ondon lodging-house and an unshaven man with sad red
es peered out suspiciously at him, as though no one ever
alled except to harass him further.

'And what did you say?' Kate asked.

'Only "Don't you know me?" ' Jimmy recited, as though
very word of it was fixed in his memory. 'And he said,
You have the advantage of me." So I said, "I'm your
on." '

'Oh, my!' Kate exclaimed, profoundly impressed and a
ttle sorry for Jimmy's father, though she had resolved to
ate everything she learned about him. 'And what did he say
en?'

'He just started to cry.'

'Fitter for him do it fifteen years ago!' Kate shouted in a
udden access of rage.

'I said, "Well, it's all over and done with now", and he
id, " 'Tisn't, nor 'twill never be. Your mother missed
othing when she missed me. I was a curse to others, and
ow I'm only a curse to myself." '

'How sorry he is for himself!' said Kate.

'He has reason,' said Jimmy, and went on to describe the
qualid room where he had stayed for a week with his
ather, sleeping in the same unmade bed, going out with him
o the pub to put a few shillings on a horse, yet Kate felt a
ttle touch of pride in the way Jimmy described the sudden
utbursts of extravagant humour that lit up his father's
aaudlin self-pity. And then, being Jimmy, he could not help
aughing outright at the good advice which was all his
ather had to give him – warnings against drink and betting,
ut mostly against being untrue to himself.

'The cheek of him!' cried Kate, who could see nothing in
ne least humorous in it. 'Oh, that 'tis me he should have
ad! I'd soon give him his answer, the night-walking vaga-
ond!'

'I don't care,' Jimmy said with a defiant shrug of his shoulders. 'I like him.'

Kate could scarcely reply to this, it was so unjust. She was furious at the thought that after all her years with Jimmy she might have lost him in a single day to the man who had never raised a finger to help him, nor asked whether he was living or dead. But she knew, too, that it was fear that made her angry, because she had gone closer to losing Jimmy than she had ever done before.

5

At first, when Jimmy got a girl of his own, Kate paid no attention. She thought it was only foolishness, but when it went on for more than six months, and Jimmy took the girl out every Friday night, she began to grow nervous. She told Mrs Sumners that she was afraid Jimmy might marry 'beneath him'. When this got back to the girl's people, they were outraged, because they were afraid that Mary was going to do the same thing. 'A boy that nobody knows who he is or where he comes from!' they went around saying. 'Or is she in her right mind at all?'

Kate dreaded Friday evenings on that account. Jimmy would come in from work, and shave and strip and wash under the tap in the backyard. Then he would change into his best blue suit and put Brilliantine on his hair, and she watched every move he made with gloom and resentment.

'You're not going to be late again?' she would ask.

'Why wouldn't I be late?' Jimmy would ask.

'You know I can't sleep while you do be out.' (This was true; any other night of the week she had no trouble in sleeping.)

Finally James ticked her off. One Friday evening he closed his book, raised his glasses on his forehead, and said 'Granny, you worry too much about Jimmy and that girl. Jimmy is steadier than you give him credit for.'

'He is, I hear,' she retorted rudely. 'He have as much sense as you have, and that's not much, God knows. Wouldn't you go out and have a game of handball like a natural boy?'

'That has nothing to do with it,' James said equably. 'I know Jimmy better than you do. There's nothing wrong with Jimmy only that he has very little confidence in himself, and he's too easily influenced. That's why he prefers to go with stupid people instead of clever ones. They make him feel superior. But he has a very good intelligence if he ever tries to make use of it.'

At the same time Kate wondered often if Jimmy would ever outgrow his attitude to his family. So far as his immediate neighbours were concerned, the whole thing was forgotten except to his credit. He was as much one of themselves as any of the honest transactions brought up in the locality. But it was as if Jimmy himself could never really forget that he was an outsider; again and again the old fever broke out in him, and each time the form it took came as a surprise to Kate. Once he took off on his bicycle to a little town eighty miles away where his uncle ran a grocery store. His uncle had kept his father supplied with small money-orders that promptly went on horses. Jimmy didn't get much of a welcome because his uncle quite unjustly suspected that Jimmy wanted money-orders as well, and, besides, he did not want the job of explaining his nephew to the townspeople. In spite of his tepid welcome, Jimmy came home in high spirits and gave Kate and James a really funny description of his uncle; a frightened, cadaverous, clever little man, who lectured Jimmy on the way the country was going to the dogs, with people neglecting religion, working less and expecting more. Jimmy felt he had the laugh on his uncle, but at Christmas it was his uncle who had the laugh on Jimmy, because he sent him a small money-order as well. Jimmy was deeply touched by it; once or twice they saw him take it out of his pocket and study it with a smile as though it were a long and intimate letter.

Worse still, there was the summer when he took his bicycle and, with the help of his sailor friend, stowed away again on the Fishguard boat. This time he cycled through southern England to the little Dorset town where his mother had lodged while she was having him, all alone, without husband, lover, or friend to encourage her. Kate thought this whole expedition very queer and grumbled again that he was 'never right', but somewhere inside herself she realized that it was part of his way of getting to belong. And she knew, whatever anyone said, he would go on like that to the end of his days, pursued by the dream of a normal life that he might have lived and a normal family he might have grown up with.

James observed it too, with considerable interest, but with a fundamental disapproval. He had never shown much curiosity about his own blood-relations, though he knew he had brothers and sisters who went to expensive English schools, and he let it be seen that he thought Jimmy cheapened himself by the way he sought out his own.

'Ah, that's only because I always had to live too close to them,' Jimmy said. 'Boy, if I was like you, I'd never have anything to do with any of them again.'

'Oh, I don't know,' James grumbled. 'I don't see why I should avoid them. I'd like to meet my mother and my brothers and sisters. It's only natural, but I don't want to meet them yet.'

'You're right, boy,' Jimmy said with sudden depression. 'Because all they'd do is look down on you. Oh, they'll be polite and all the rest of it, but they'll look down on you just the same.'

'Oh, you always take things to the fair,' James said petulantly. 'You think people look down on you because you haven't enough confidence in yourself. You always think there's something wrong with you, and it's not that at all. It's something wrong with them. They're people who pay far too much attention to what other people think. If I meet them when I'm a civil servant or a teacher in the university they'll be delighted to know me. People like that never neglect anyone who may be of use to them.'

Kate, amused by James' juvenile lecturing, knew that there was a sad wisdom in what he said. While Jimmy, who had something of his father's weakness and charm, might prove a liability, James would work and save, and it would be his curiosity about his family that would be satisfied, not theirs about him. And James would make perfectly certain that no member of it patronized him. She was very old, and her grip on life had slackened, but she did very much long to see how James would deal with his family.

All the same, she knew she wouldn't see it. She fell ill again and Molly came to the house to nurse her, while Nora and usually one or both of their husbands came to relieve her in the evenings. Her presence made an immediate change in the house. She was swift and efficient; she fed the boys and made conversation with callers, leaning against the doorpost with folded arms, and then would slip away into the front room or out the yard and weep savagely to herself for a few minutes, as another woman might do for a quick drink. The priest came, and Molly chatted with him about the affairs of the parish as though she had no other thought in mind, and then dashed up to her mother's room again. Kate asked to see Jimmy and James. The two boys went quietly up the stairs and stood at either side of the big bed. Each of them took one of her hands.

'Don't upset yeerselves too much, boys,' she said. 'I know ye'll miss me, but ye need have no regrets. Ye were the two best sons a mother ever reared.' She thought hard for a moment and added something that shocked them all. 'I'm proud of ye, and yeer father is proud of ye.'

'Mammy!' Molly whispered urgently. 'You forget. 'Tis Jimmy and James.'

Kate opened her eyes for a few moments and looked straight at her.

'I know well who it is,' she said. Then her eyes closed again and she breathed noisily for some minutes, as though she were trying to recollect herself. 'Don't do anything he'd be ashamed of. He was a good man and a clean-living man, and he never robbed anyone of a ha'penny. Jimmy, look after your little brother for me.'

'I will, Mammy,' Jimmy said through his tears.

Something about that sudden reversion to the language of childhood made Molly break down. She took refuge in the front room to weep. Nora scolded her as all the Mahoneys had always scolded one another.

'Ah, have a bit of sense, girl!' she said lightly. 'You know yourself poor Mammy's mind is wandering.'

'It is not wandering, Nora,' Molly said hysterically. 'I saw her and you didn't. She knew what she was saying, and Jimmy knew it too. They were her real children all the time, and we were only the outsiders.'

That night, when Kate was quiet at last in her brown shroud, clutching the rosary beads on her breast, the neighbours came in and sat round her in the candlelight. They were asking the same question that Molly had already asked herself: how it was that a woman so old could take the things the world had thrown away and from them fashion a new family, dearer to her than the old and better than any she had known. But Kate had taken her secret with her.

(1960)

Frank O'Connor

The Mad Lomasneys and other stories 80p

'Brilliant and penetrating studies of young men who are either agin the government or agin religion, young women who have a struggle between their good Catholic consciences and sex, or priests who have to struggle with both'
OXFORD MAIL

Walter Macken

One of Ireland's greatest novelists. 'Where the writer knows and loves his country as Walter Macken does, there is warmth and life'
TIMES LITERARY SUPPLEMENT

Brown Lord of the Mountain 90p

Donn Donnschleibhe returns to his home village bringing new life, marvellous changes — and revenge

Rain on the Wind £1.25

A rich, racy story of the fisherfolk of Galway — of fighting and drinking, of hurling and poaching, of weddings and wakes.

The Bogman £1.50

Tricked into marriage to the sexless, middle-aged Julia, Cahal's heart is lost to the wanton Maire, and his rebellion grows.

Lewis Grassic Gibbon
A Scots Quair £2.95

From the years of the Great War to the hungry thirties, Lewis Grassic Gibbon's magnificent trilogy spans the life of a woman and the story of a people. This powerful saga of Scottish life through three decades is now published in one volume.

'His three great novels have the impetus and music of mountain burns in full spate' OBSERVER

Jean Stubbs
The Ironmaster £1.75

Three children were born to Ned and Dorcas Howarth of Kit's Hill, high on the Pennines. Charlotte, strong-willed wife of a London radical, was robbed of her man by death and brought back to Kit's Hill. Sturdy Dick, born to inherit his father's farm, would wait for the good and golden harvest that never comes. But bright young William, now master of his own forge, had his eyes fixed on the future: in the dawn of industrial England, he was the Howarth destined for greatness, a man born to be ironmaster.

Wilkie Collins
The Woman in White £1.95

'A solitary woman, dressed from head to foot in white garments ...

From the moment of Walter Hartright's strange encounter on a moonlit Hampstead Heath, the reader is caught up in the spell of Wilkie Collins' gripping narrative and driven on to the end of a novel that stands as one of the greatest mystery thrillers in the language.

Fiction

☐	**Options**	Freda Bright	£1.50p
☐	**The Thirty-nine Steps**	John Buchan	£1.25p
☐	**Secret of Blackoaks**	Ashley Carter	£1.50p
☐	**A Night of Gaiety**	Barbara Cartland	90p
☐	**The Sittaford Mystery**	Agatha Christie	£1.00p
☐	**Dupe**	Liza Cody	£1.25p
☐	**Lovers and Gamblers**	Jackie Collins	£2.25p
☐	**Sphinx**	Robin Cook	£1.25p
☐	**Ragtime**	E. L. Doctorow	£1.50p
☐	**Rebecca**	Daphne du Maurier	£1.75p
☐	**Flashman**	George Macdonald Fraser	£1.50p
☐	**The Moneychangers**	Arthur Hailey	£1.95p
☐	**Secrets**	Unity Hall	£1.50p
☐	**The Maltese Falcon**	Dashiell Hammett	95p
☐	**Simon the Coldheart**	Georgette Heyer	95p
☐	**The Eagle Has Landed**	Jack Higgins	£1.75p
☐	**The Master Sniper**	Stephen Hunter	£1.50p
☐	**Smiley's People**	John le Carré	£1.75p
☐	**To Kill a Mockingbird**	Harper Lee	£1.50p
☐	**The Empty Hours**	Ed McBain	£1.25p
☐	**Gone with the Wind**	Margaret Mitchell	£2.95p
☐	**The Totem**	Tony Morrell	£1.25p
☐	**Platinum Logic**	Tony Parsons	£1.75p
☐	**Rage of Angels**	Sidney Sheldon	£1.75p
☐	**The Unborn**	David Shobin	£1.50p
☐	**A Town Like Alice**	Nevile Shute	£1.50p
☐	**A Falcon Flies**	Wilbur Smith	£1.95p
☐	**The Deep Well at Noon**	Jessica Stirling	£1.75p
☐	**The Ironmaster**	Jean Stubbs	£1.75p
☐	**The Music Makers**	E. V. Thompson	£1.50p

Non-fiction

☐	**Extraterrestrial Civilizations**	Isaac Asimov	£1.50p
☐	**Pregnancy**	Gordon Bourne	£2.95p
☐	**Out of Practice**	Rob Buckman	95p
☐	**The 35mm Photographer's Handbook**	Julian Calder and John Garrett	£5.95p
☐	**Travellers' Britain**	Arthur Eperon	£2.95p
☐	**Travellers' Italy**		£2.95p
☐	**The Complete Calorie Counter**	Eileen Fowler	70p

☐	**The Diary of Anne Frank**	Anne Frank	£1.25p
☐	**Linda Goodman's Sun Signs**	Linda Goodman	£1.95p
☐	**Mountbatten**	Richard Hough	£1.95p
☐	**How to be a Gifted Parent**	David Lewis	£1.95p
☐	**Symptoms**	Sigmund Stephen Miller	£2.50p
☐	**Book of Worries**	Robert Morley	£1.50p
☐	**The Hangover Handbook**	David Outerbridge	£1.25p
☐	**The Alternative Holiday Catalogue**	edited by Harriet Peacock	£1.95p
☐	**The Pan Book of Card Games**	Hubert Phillips	£1.50p
☐	**Food for All the Family**	Magnus Pyke	£1.50p
☐	**Everything Your Doctor Would Tell You If He Had the Time**	Claire Rayner	£4.95p
☐	**Just Off for the Weekend**	John Slater	£2.50p
☐	**An Unfinished History of the World**	Hugh Thomas	£3.95p
☐	**The Third Wave**	Alvin Toffler	£1.95p
☐	**The Flier's Handbook**		£5.95p

All these books are available at your local bookshop or newsagent, or can be ordered direct from the publisher. Indicate the number of copies required and fill in the form below

5

....

Name_____
(Block letters please)

Address_____

_____

Send to Pan Books (CS Department), Cavaye Place, London SW10 9PG
Please enclose remittance to the value of the cover price plus:
35p for the first book plus 15p per copy for each additional book ordered
to a maximum charge of £1.25 to cover postage and packing
Applicable only in the UK

While every effort is made to keep prices low, it is sometimes
necessary to increase prices at short notice. Pan Books reserve
the right to show on covers and charge new retail prices which
may differ from those advertised in the text or elsewhere